Matthew's Tangled Trails

A Books by Teens Adventure

By

Jeri Fink and Donna Paltrowitz

This book is a work of fiction. Although characters and the authors may have circumstances in common, none of the actions or events is based on real events in the authors' lives. Names, characters, places and incidents either are the product of the authors' imaginations or are used fictitiously. Any resemblance to actual events or persons living or dead is entirely coincidental. Although the author and publisher have made every effort to ensure the accuracy and completeness of information contained in this book, we assume no responsibility for errors, inaccuracies, omissions, or any inconsistency herein. Any slights of people, places or organizations are unintentional.

ISBN 0-9716567-2-X

Matthew's Tangled Trails
Jeri Fink and Donna Paltrowitz

Book design by Jeremy Ryan
www.retne.com

Printed and Available at:
Book Web Publishing, Ltd.
2952 Judith Drive
Bellmore, NY 11710
516-221-3850
www.bookwebpublishing.com

A wish for my budding authors:

Set your standards high
Believe in yourself
Always try your hardest
And you will never lose.
Expand your minds
And follow your dreams.

Broaden your horizons
And reach for the stars
You won't need a ladder -
Just delve into the unknown
With high expectations
for you are our future.

Mrs. Ellen Schwartz

We believe that teenagers are the best-equipped people to talk about their lives and worlds. Consequently, Books by Teens is designed to incorporate their voices, experiences, insights, and ideas in every book we write. Each novel invites teenagers through schools across the country to participate in the writing, editing, designing, reviewing, and promoting of their book. All participants write a dedication. Please take a moment to read what they have to say about their work.
Thank you for listening to the teens.

Jeri Fink and Donna Paltrowitz

Matthew's Tangled Trails

is dedicated to Bellmore-Merrick CHSD.
Their commitment to the children of Bellmore-Merrick combines creativity and academic excellence to enable exceptional teachers, such as Mrs. Ellen Schwartz, to provide an exciting and innovative educational experience.

To Mrs. Ellen Schwartz and Mr. Sean Llewellyn who, with enthusiasm, creativity, and determination made Matthew's Tangled Trails a reality.

To all the kids from Mrs. Ellen Schwartz's 7th grade Honors who shared their ideas, debated the issues, and brought Matthew to life.

Special thanks to:

Adam Paltrowitz, whose conducting abilities strengthened our voices.
Dr. Walter C. Woolley, who provided the original spark.
Ellen Schwartz, for her superlative teaching and editing skills.
Gizmo, for being our favorite labradoodle.
Jeremy Ryan, for his amazing artistry and technical advice.
Richard Fink, for his unquestioning faith in our work.
Russell Fink, for bringing us the best of media.
Stacey Becker for sharing her knowledge of children and their literature.

Borders Bookstore in Westbury, New York for welcoming Merrick Avenue Middle School student-authors.

To our husbands, Rick and Stuart, our children, David, Russell, Adam, Yvonne, Darren and Shari who supply the clues to our daily mysteries.

To the special seniors in our lives, Larry Milman, Harvey and Edna Fink, Robin March, Alice and Murray Paltrowitz, Dora Eisenstein, and Herbert Michelson, who leaped generations to wander through Matthew's Tangled Trails.

To our families and friends who share in all of Matthew's webs.

Thanks for your support!

In loving memory of Gladys Milman, Ruth Roth, Judy Becker, and Persis Burlingame.

Dedications from Merrick Avenue Middle School

Abby Cohen	To my family, friends, and Mrs. Schwartz.
Allison Saltzman	To all of the men and women, including my father, who worked for Marsh MC in Tower One of the World Trade Centers.
Amanda Burnett	I dedicate this to my family and friends.
Amanda Pechman	To my mom, dad and brother, Matthew.
Andrew Bank	To my parents - I love you.
Arielle Richheimer	To my family and friends.
Bennett Siegel	To my friends, family, and English Teacher.
Brian Tannenbaum	To Grandma Janet, Papa Marty, Papa Elmer, Grandma Edna and Grandma Lynn. I love you guys very much.
Brittany Clahane	I would like to dedicate this book to my sisters, Sarah and Megan, and my friends.
Brittany Neely	To the 9-11 victims, heroes, and their families.
Bryan Brown	To my supportive family.
Caitlin Isham	To my family, friends, and all of those who have helped me along the way.
Cesar A. Gonzalez	To all the Hispanic people that work hard to succeed in life.
Chelsea Fitzgerald	To everyone who lost someone on September 11th and to my parents and sister, Ava, with love.
Christine Berghorn	I dedicate this to my family and friends.
Courtney Siegel	To all the 9-11 victims and heroes as well as their families.
Dalia Gaon	I dedicate this book to my family and friends.
Danielle Schwarz	I would like to dedicate this book to my family and friends.
Doug Witzenbocker	I dedicate this book to my family for helping me through everything and always supporting me.
Douglas Gibbons	To my friends and family.
Evan Massa	Thanks to all my friends and family!

Flynn Hill	To the 9/11 victims, friends, and family.
Hailey Simon	To my family, friends, and Yogi.
Haleigh Lester	To my family and friends.
Ian Li	To my family and my two cousins, Chris and Chad.
Jason Shilling	I dedicate Matthew's Tangled Trails to my family and friends.
John O'Sullivan	I dedicate this to my dog, family, and friends.
Jordan Schneider	I'd like to dedicate this book to my family, including my Guinea Pig.
Jordan Wolfson	To my loving parents.
Julie Mintz	To my family, friends, and IHC girls.
Katherine L. DiMaggio	To my friends and family, especially C.J. and to Mrs. Schwartz.
Kelly McCarthy	To my friends and family, who have helped me throughout my life.
Kimberly Gurock	To my family, my sisters Danielle, Tracy, and Lisa, and my friends.
Landon Marder	To my family and my teacher, Mrs. Schwartz for making this possible.
Laura Lupo	To my mom, my dad, my sister Catherine, Lucy, and my best friend Jenna Sacks.
Lauren Williams	To my parents.
Lindsay Melworm	I dedicate this book to my family, friends and to my English teacher, Mrs. Schwartz, who without her, we wouldn't have done this book.
Lisa Gurock	To my loving family.
Loretta C. Jacobs	I dedicate this to my mom and dad, but especially to my brother David, who overcame bullying and didn't let it get this serious. I love my family.
Matt Cohen	To my family, may they always make the right choices.
Max Levy	For my mom, my dad, and my sister.
Michael George	I dedicate this book to my family and friends.
Michael Greenbaum	To all my family, friends, and my cat, "Paws."
Michelle Kremer	I dedicate this to my family and friends who allow me to live in such a protected world. Thanks!

Mike Karp	To my mom and dad.
Mike Monteverde	To my friends, family, and whoever reads this book!!
Mitchell Kochman	To my mom, Susan, my dad Ron, and my sister Rikki.
Nicole Taykhman	To my mom, dad, and sister Diana.
Rebecca Vedrin	Thank you to my family and all of my friends! You guys are the best!
Sean Keegan	To my parents, my sister Breanna, and my friends, Brendan, Mike, and Roshan.
Shaun Werbelow	To all my family and friends for helping me in times of need.
Sofia-Marie Gutilla	To my friends, family, and English teachers.
Stuart Rubinstein	To all the people lost on the attack of the World Trade Center.
Zach Coppola	To my mom.
Zack Ehrlich	To my family.

Mary Truelson	To Brian C. Hickey, FDNY-R4 "The heavens themselves blaze forth the death of princes." - William Shakespeare

Mrs. Schwartz	This is dedicated to all of my seventh grade students who hold the gift of bright futures filled with promises of great things to come.

Internet Glossary

AWGTHTGTTA	Are we going to have to go through that again?
bbl	be back later
bbr	burnt beyond repair
b4	before
b4n	bye for now
btw	by the way
c	see
.edu	extension in web address to indicate educational institution
g2g	got to go
lol	laughing out loud
morf	male OR female
ne 1	anyone
nsn	never say never
omg	Oh my God
r	are
rite	right
rotfl	rolling on the floor laughing
tnx	thanks
u r	you are
u	you
vbf	very big frown
vbg	very big grin
w/e	whatever
y	why
1	one
2	to, too, two
4	for, four
:-)	smiley face
:-(	frown
:-0	wow
;-0	wink

Table of Contents

Matthew's Tangled Trails

Illustration Credit: Mitchell Kochman

The Rhodes Reverie

Monday, March 15

Welcome to the Rhodes Middle School online bulletin board. Post your ideas, thoughts, and adventures! Leave messages for friends and talk about your favorite classes!

>**MISSING MATH HOMEWORK DUE WEDNESDAY** Who did the homework and wants to give me answers?

>Can you imagine getting kicked out of school for copying off the internet? Wanna protest?

>Social studies paper due Friday. All students are responsible for the most important research paper of the year. Don't forget Friday, March 19. Mr. Richie

>Kids who are "different" are being discriminated against and their self-esteem is being lowered

>Lost left shoe! Don't know how I missed it.

Chapter One
Bite and Run

"Gizmo," Eddie grimaced, "what kind of name is that for a dog?"

Matthew aimed and took a shot. The three boys watched as the basketball curved into the air and fell through the net, never touching the backboard.

"He's not just a dog," Matthew said, pleased with himself. He laughed at the antics of the curly-haired puppy. "He's a labradoodle."

The ball hit the driveway. Before they could reach it, Gizmo was barking and chasing as if it was a howling cat. Eddie looked at Matthew. Eddie's brown skin glistened with sweat even though it was only March and still cool outside. Eddie had just begun playing basketball with the guys. Gizmo barked again in a high-pitched puppy roar, bringing Matthew's attention back to the boys.

"What's a labradoodle?" Eddie asked, laughing at the dog.

"Yeah, what's a labradoodle?" Mike insisted, squaring his large shoulders and flexing his biceps. Mike was big and ripped, and most kids in the school made sure not to disagree with anything he said or did. They all knew that Mike loved to pick on kids smaller, younger, or weaker than he. It was easy to become Mike's target - a position no one wanted to play.

"My mom's friend owns Gizmo," Matthew explained. "She's a family therapist and is training him. While she's out-of-town, I'm getting paid to puppy-sit. It's an easy way to make money." He glanced down at Gizmo. "To answer your question, labradoodles are special dogs that are supposed to be able to help people. They come from Australia."

"Help people?" Eddie asked.

"You know, therapy dogs." Matthew grinned, "Gizmo is going to be a therapy dog and help people to feel better when he grows up. He'll go to hospitals, schools, nursing homes, and those kinds of places. They even had therapy dogs helping rescue workers and families after the attack on the World Trade Center in New York."

The chocolate-colored, curly-haired puppy leaped on the basketball and rolled over, suddenly finding himself with his back on the driveway. He yelped loudly.

"Give me a break," Mike laughed. "He doesn't look very special to me. He doesn't even look like he could help anyone. Yeah, that mutt looks like he could use some help himself. "

Matthew shrugged. "Want to play another game?"

"Sure," Eddie said quickly.

Matthew jogged over to Gizmo and reached for the basketball.

He would always wonder about what happened next.

Gizmo didn't bark or whimper or growl. He just looked into Matthew's eyes as if something was seriously askew. It was only a brief moment, yet Matthew knew it wasn't his imagination.

Matthew playfully wrenched the basketball from Gizmo.

"Let's play," Matthew shouted to Mike and Eddie.

They hesitated too. There was definitely something strange in the air.

"Let's play," Matthew repeated warily.

Behind him, Matthew could hear Gizmo scurrying to his feet. He seemed to be ready to play with the boys, but wavered and headed in the opposite direction. Matthew didn't see it at first. He only saw Mike and Eddie watching the puppy.

"He's going for my books," Mike said suddenly.

The boys had left their schoolbooks and backpacks on the grass next to the driveway.

Matthew turned around.

Gizmo was now a blur of brown fur, his gawky legs and lumbering paws propelling him towards Mike's books. His skinny puppy-tail stretched out straight behind him, and his long ears flapped in the wind.

"He's going to tear everything apart," Mike yelled contemptuously.

Gizmo reached the books first. He grabbed a mouthful of papers and ran. Mike chased him while Eddie laughed.

Matthew didn't think it was funny. Gizmo was staying with him and Mom for a few weeks. This was the first time he had done anything destructive. Matthew quivered. There was something very wrong with the whole scene.

"I'm going to make sure that mutt doesn't get into my books," Eddie grinned. He walked over to the grass and reached down to gather his stuff. Matthew couldn't move.

Eddie gathered his books and papers. "I don't believe it," he mumbled, "Gizmo snatched my stuff, not Mike's."

Eddie stared at the papers in his hands.

Matthew watched as if in a movie theater.

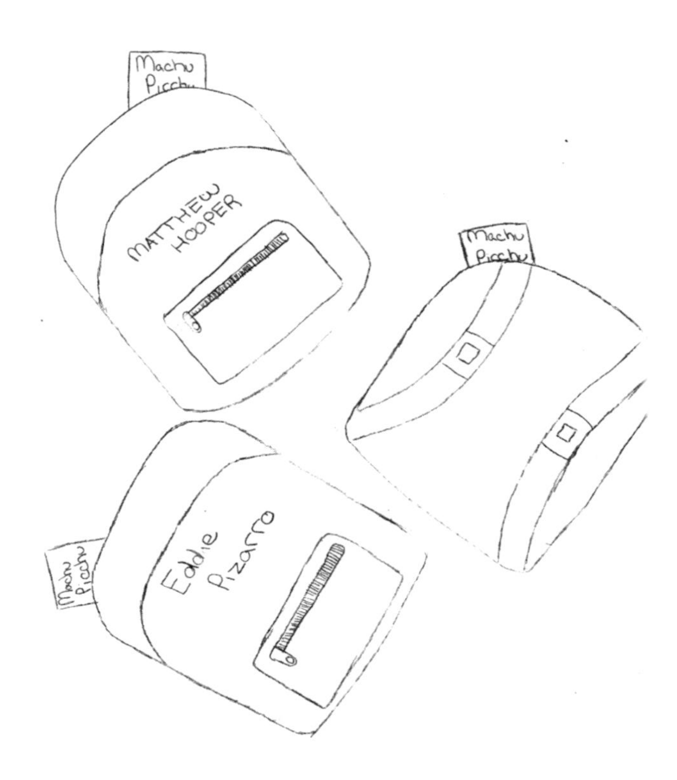

Illustration Credit: Mitchell Kochman

Mike reached Gizmo and yanked the papers out of the puppy's mouth. Then he stopped and like Eddie, stared at the papers in his hands.

Matthew glanced at Gizmo.

The puppy opened his mouth in a doggy grin, looking very proud of himself.

Suddenly Matthew knew he had to gather his own schoolbooks and papers. He reached for his leather backpack when he heard Eddie's words.

"I don't believe this is happening. How did Mike get my paper?"

They were words that Matthew would think about over and over again in the ensuing days.

Mike tore back to the two boys. "What is *this* about?" Mike waved some papers in the air.

Eddie stared at him blankly.

"It was you," Mike roared at Eddie. "I should have known it was you."

"What are you talking about?" Eddie's eyes blazed. "You stole my paper."

Mike inched closer to Eddie. Mike's fists were balled and Eddie cowered. Matthew knew that Eddie was in big trouble.

Matthew felt the blood drain from his face. He pushed his way between Mike and Eddie.

"What's going on?"

Eddie took a deep breath. "You know the paper about South America that we have to write for social studies," his voice was subdued, "the one Mr. Richie assigned over a month ago?"

Matthew knew a lot about that paper. He was in Mr. Richie's class, along with Mike, Eddie, and most of the basketball team. Mr. Richie assigned the paper more than a month before it was due to make sure they did serious research. Anyone who received a grade higher than 90 was excused from taking the final exam.

"I *need* that 90," Eddie continued. "I want to keep my grades up and if I have more time to study for my other finals, I'll be able to try out for the varsity basketball team . . ."

"Is that why you sold it?" Mike asked incredulously. He stepped around Matthew to directly face Eddie.

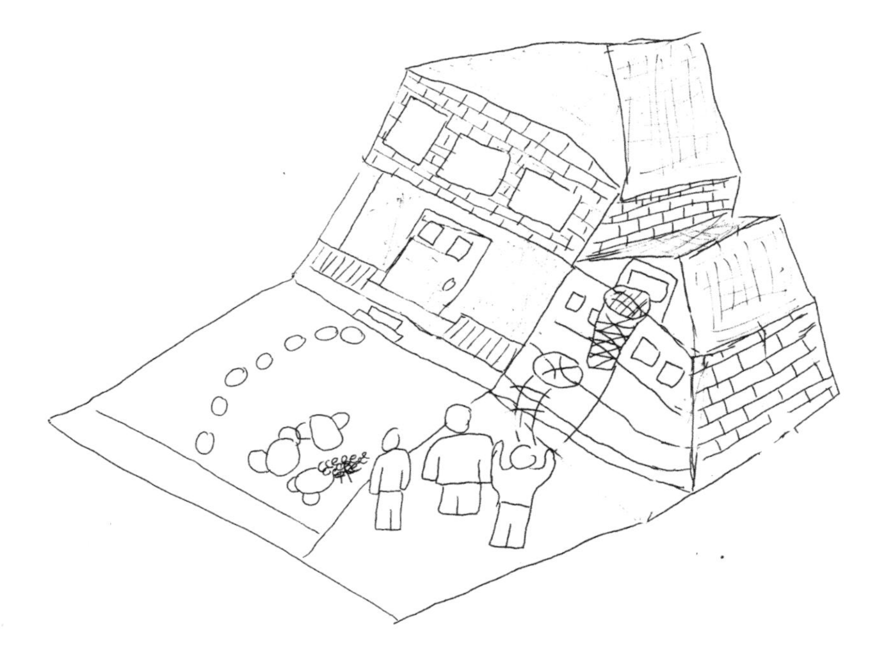

Illustration Credit: Max Levy

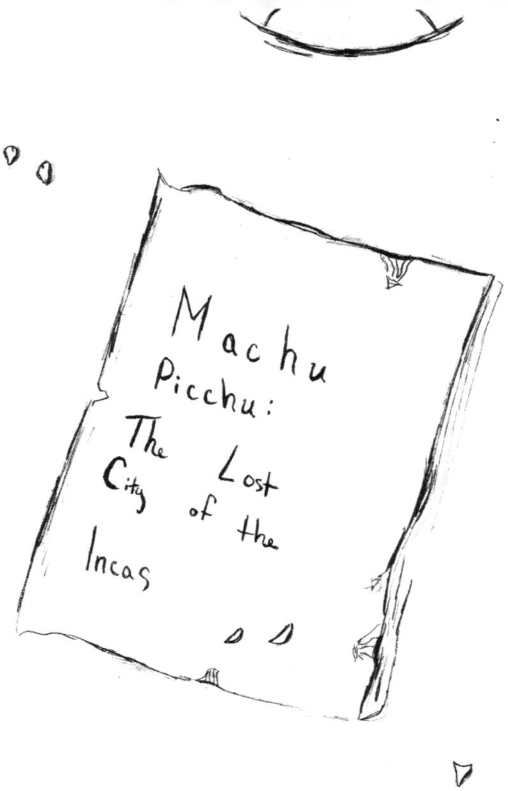

Illustration Credit: Mike Monteverde

"What are you talking about?" Eddie's voice faltered.

"Sold it?" Matthew whispered.

"Yeah," Mike turned to Matthew. "I bought my paper on the internet. Somebody e-mailed me and said they would sell it to me for $30. It was a guaranteed 90." He glared at Eddie.

Eddie was speechless.

"Can I see your papers?" Matthew asked.

Mike handed him Eddie's paper, complete with puppy tooth marks.

Eddie handed him Mike's paper.

They were identical.

Machu Picchu: The Lost City of the Incas.

Matthew reached into his leather backpack and pulled out his social studies paper. His hands were trembling.

Matthew's paper was identical to the other two. Mr. Richie's assignment instructed them to write *anything* on the subject of South America. They could research countries or cities, people or political parties. Who would have ever thought of Machu Picchu? It seemed so remote when Matthew got the e-mail. He was convinced that there wouldn't be any other papers on the lost Incan city. It only cost thirty dollars out of his puppy-sitting money for a paper that guaranteed being waived from the final. The offer was too good to be true.

Matthew recalled the classic internet adage: If it's too good to be true, it probably isn't.

Mike sneered. "So smart boy bought his paper off the internet, too?"

"Why do you think I'm puppy-sitting?" Matthew asked, glaring at Eddie. "I got an e-mail saying that I could have the perfect paper for Mr. Richie's class so I wouldn't have to take the final. Guaranteed to get me that 90. So I bought it. I left thirty dollars in my mailbox, and the next day the paper was delivered to me online. The thirty dollars was gone. I was going to turn it in Friday, on time."

"Cost me thirty dollars too," Mike added.

They turned to Eddie.

"Eduardo Pizarro," Mike spat out his name, "you owe me thirty bucks."

Eddie opened his mouth to object.

"Wait," Matthew stopped him. "Eddie, did you write this paper?"

Eddie nodded.

"Did you sell this paper?"

"No way! Why would I sell the same paper that I was going to turn in? I can prove I wrote it - here's the disk where I did all my editing." Eddie started searching through his backpack.

"Where's the disk?" Mike heckled him.

"It's right . . ." Eddie looked at Matthew blankly.

"Eddie?" Matthew asked.

"It's gone," Eddie said hoarsely. "My disk is gone. I don't know what happened to it . . . I even had an article on it for *The Rhodes Reporter*. I hope they saved my hard copy.

"Yeah, right," Mike snarled. "You expect us to believe you lost the disk with your paper on it? Do you really think we're *that* stupid? After all, you're Hispanic. You can sell your paper and write another one about South America in a second."

"What do you mean?"

"It's like writing your name, Pizarro. You don't have to work hard at stuff like that. You just know it."

"My grandparents and my father are from El Salvador," Eddie

struggled to explain. "My mother, sister, and I were born right here. I don't know any more about South America than you."

"Sure. That's why you have a Spanish name."

"That has nothing to do with . . ."

Once again, Matthew wedged himself between the two boys. "You say," Matthew took a deep breath, "that you wrote the paper but didn't sell it?"

"I would never sell a paper!" Eddie's eyes pleaded.

"Liar . . ." Mike bellowed. "Just like your disk disappeared into thin air. You'll say anything to get out of it! Maybe Gizmo ate it?"

"Enough," Matthew shouted even louder. "Right now we don't know the truth."

"I know the truth," Mike sneered. "This guy is a lying cheat and a thief." He grabbed his papers and books. "You better think again about who you hang out with, Matthew. I'm out of here."

Mike turned and stomped down the street.

Eddie and Matthew stared at his back.

"I didn't do it," Eddie said softly. "You have to believe me."

"You didn't do what?" Matthew demanded. "You didn't write the paper or you didn't sell it? Which one?"

Eddie bent down and gathered the rest of his books. "It always comes down to the same thing, right? If Mike said he didn't sell the paper, you would believe him. But me? I'm Hispanic and the new kid in school, so it has to be me."

"Wait . . . I didn't say that . . ."

Eddie glanced at him. "You didn't have to, Matthew."

Eddie turned and walked away in the opposite direction from Mike.

The only one left was Gizmo. Matthew didn't know whether to stare at Mike, Eddie, or Gizmo.

The puppy won. Gizmo gazed sadly at Matthew.

"You know, Gizmo," Matthew said to the dog. "It's bad enough we all know Mike is a bully. Now we have a new bully and he's online. We can't even see his face." Matthew shrugged. "I guess you might call him an e-bully." Matthew laughed. "What happens now?"

Gizmo had no answer.

Matthew folded the paper and jammed it into his pocket.

Suddenly he heard the sound of a basketball on the pavement. Before he could even turn around to see where it was coming from, Gizmo took off.

"Gizmo!" Matthew yelled, but the puppy was too fast.

Gizmo tore across the driveway, over the grass, and into the street.

"No," Matthew cried, lunging for the puppy. It was futile. Gizmo was way ahead of him. Frustrated, Matthew raced after him.

Gizmo darted down the street, up a driveway, and onto the sidewalk. Matthew fought to catch his breath, furious at the dog. Matthew ran as fast as he could, as if he were in the middle of a basketball game against Grand Avenue Middle School. Matthew Hooper was a starter on the Rhodes Middle School Basketball Team. He was the tallest guy in the group, playing center on a team that had won the regional championship only a few weeks ago. He was also a really fast runner.

"Gizmo," Matthew cried, "stop!" Matthew never saw them coming. He was too busy worrying about Gizmo and what to do with the social studies paper to notice Nicole and Jenna. All of a sudden everything began to move faster. Gizmo was gaining momentum.

Matthew sprinted across the street. "Gizmo," he roared again, "stop!" He glanced down the block. The crazy bus driver in the big yellow school bus had just turned the corner, heading straight for the puppy.

Gizmo never looked back.

Illustration Credit: John O'Sullivan

Chapter Two
E-Bullied

The yellow school bus was empty, so the crazy bus driver picked up speed, tearing down the block.

He was aiming for Gizmo -- just like he always targeted the big, orange traffic- cones in front of the school.

Nicole and Jenna never noticed. They were walking home from school deeply immersed in conversation. Nicole was dribbling a basketball. She rarely went anywhere without a basketball. Nicole claimed she could think better when her basketball was in motion.

Matthew could see the crazy bus driver's face through the window. His frizzy, gray hair was standing on end, and his mouth was busy, singing his usual battle songs.

Matthew shouted louder. He wasn't sure if Gizmo didn't hear him or was just ignoring his command. Gizmo took a flying leap at the basketball, stealing it better than anyone from the Rhodes Runners Basketball Team. Nicole and Jenna stopped in surprise.

Nicole was Matthew's very best friend. He had become a good

Illustration Credit: Andrew Bank

basketball player because of her. Nicole lived right across the street from Matthew, part of a large family that was very different from his own. Matthew's parents were divorced - he was an only child living with Mom and visiting Dad on the weekends. He only had one other friend who had no brothers or sisters, Kyle Harris. Kyle had a very close cousin, where Matthew only had his friends. Nicole was the best and her house was always full of people, kids playing, and her mother's great cooking.

"No, Gizmo," Matthew pleaded with the puppy.

Gizmo wrestled the basketball, rolling over into the street.

Although Nicole was two years older than Matthew, she was closer to him than anyone else. Nicole was a sophomore starter on the high school varsity basketball team and taught him how to be a steady, solid player. She helped him figure out his problems and deal with what went on at school. Now Nicole was helping Jenna, a hotshot player on the Rhodes Middle School Girls' Basketball Team. Sometimes Matthew felt left out when the girls started talking about things like shopping and boy bands. Nicole tried to reassure Matthew by saying that she would always be there for him.

At that moment, Matthew wasn't thinking about Nicole or Jenna. He was too afraid he would lose Gizmo.

Nicole cried out. "What's *that*?"

The crazy bus driver thundered closer.

"No," Matthew shouted again. It felt like hours before he reached Gizmo and the basketball. He was sweating heavily.

What does a puppy know about the dangers of crazy bus drivers?

Matthew wasn't sure if his feet touched the ground. He flew past Nicole and Jenna, grabbed Gizmo and the basketball, and brought them to the sidewalk. Matthew fell on his back clutching Gizmo tightly. The brown ball of curly fur licked his face as Matthew struggled to recover.

The crazy bus driver came to a screeching halt. He flipped open the doors, staring at the puppy and three kids. His black eyes blazed and his unshaven cheeks trembled.

Matthew, Nicole, Jenna, and Gizmo waited in terror.

The crazy bus driver grinned, showing crooked, yellow teeth. "Darn! I always foul out on Mondays. Try again tomorrow." He rammed the doors shut, laughing hysterically.

They watched the bus clamber away right through the stop sign.

Matthew held onto Gizmo. Nicole and Jenna sat down next to him.

"What was that all about?" She asked as Gizmo leaped over and started licking her face. She laughed.

"He saved the dog's life from the crazy bus driver," Jenna giggled, petting Gizmo's head.

Matthew watched bleakly. "Hold onto that animal," he mumbled.

Nicole glared at him. "Who is this dog?"

"Gizmo," Matthew said grudgingly, "meet Nicole and Jenna."

Nicole was incredulous. "Since when do you have a dog?"

"I don't," he sat up, brushing the dirt from his shirt. "I'm puppy-sitting. One of my mom's friends owns Gizmo. She had to go away somewhere."

"Puppy-sitting?" There was a question in Jenna's eyes. "You get paid for *that*?"

"Sure," Matthew frowned. "Enough to cover . . ." he paused, "my expenses."

"You call that puppy-sitting?" Nicole reprimanded him. "Gizmo could have been killed by the crazy bus driver."

"He wasn't," Matthew mumbled.

"How much do you get paid?" Jenna asked.

"He could have gotten killed," Nicole interrupted before Matthew could respond. "Is that the way you take care of a puppy? Ever hear of a leash, Matthew? You know it's against the law to walk a dog without a leash?"

Nicole was yelling at him. Nicole *never* yelled at Matthew. That was the way she talked to her little sister Ashley. Matthew remembered the time Ashley had run into him with a big order of fries and stained his shirt red with ketchup. *That* had been the beginning of a whole different set of problems.

"I wasn't walking him," Matthew defended himself. "We were playing basketball on my driveway when Eddie and Mike had this argument and . . ."

"What an easy job," Jenna sighed. "I wish I could puppy-sit instead of babysitting. Little kids are difficult to watch."

No one heard her.

Nicole cuddled Gizmo. "Playing basketball with a dog?"

Matthew shrugged. "It's weird. Gizmo likes basketball."

Nicole laughed. "Then he must be my kind of dog."

Nicole was no longer angry. She was actually laughing. Matthew wondered why she calmed down so quickly. *Maybe it's Gizmo*, he thought. He stared at the puppy. After all, it was Gizmo who started the whole thing by stealing Eddie's paper . . .

Matthew shook his head. "Listen, Nicole, as long as you're here, I need to speak to you."

"Sure," Nicole said, her head buried in Gizmo's curls.

"I have a problem."

"Amazing," Nicole grinned. "Problems always seem to find *you*. What now?"

Matthew took the paper from his pocket. He handed it to Nicole. He glanced nervously at Jenna. "You can't talk about this to anyone, ok?"

Jenna nodded her head vigorously. "Of course, I won't."

Unexpectedly, Gizmo settled down. He curled up in Nicole's lap and laid his head on her knees.

"What's this?" Nicole asked.

"A paper."

"I see that. It's about Machu Picchu. What's Machu Picchu?"

"The Lost City of the Incas."

"So?"

"It's a paper for social studies. Mr. Richie made a deal with us. He assigned the paper more than a month ago and told us that if we get higher than a 90, we won't have to take the final exam."

"Yeah," Jenna said complacently. "I'm in Mr. Richie's second period class. It's a great deal. He gave us more than enough time to do a good job."

"Lucky for both of you."

"No, not lucky."

"Why?"

"Because . . ." Matthew said slowly. "Mike bought this paper on the internet. Someone sent him an e-mail guaranteeing an "A" paper and . . . well, think about it. There was *so much* going on, who had time to write a paper? It was a lot easier to buy it off the internet . . ."

Nicole shook her head. "What would you expect from Mike? He's infantile enough to think that he can get away with that kind of thing. Yeah sure, we all want to take shortcuts. Get real. You know how easy it is to get caught buying a paper off the internet?" She wrinkled her nose. "It's just a stupid thing to do."

Matthew paused. "There's a bigger problem," he said finally.

"A bigger problem?"

"Yeah. Eddie has the same paper."

Nicole shook her head. Matthew and Nicole were together when they first met Eddie only two weeks ago. Matthew's mom taught History of Television at the college, so he often went there to practice basketball. Eddie Pizarro had just moved into faculty housing at Rhodes Community College. His father taught Spanish Literature at the community college, and his mother was a nurse at the health center. Eddie came here from a city school, leaving behind a spot on the basketball team and the position of Editor-in-Chief on his school newspaper. He entered Rhodes Middle School at the worst time of year - right after basketball season. Matthew had seen Eddie in his social studies classes but never bothered talking to the new kid.

Nicole and Matthew had been shooting hoops at Rhodes Community College when they noticed Eddie watching them. Nicole dribbled the ball right past Matthew, turning away at the precise moment he lunged to steal it. Laughing, Nicole swished the ball straight through the net.

"Sweet," Nicole had shouted.

"Sweet," Eddie had shouted too, unable to contain himself.

Nicole and Matthew had stopped playing to stare at him.

"Sorry," Eddie said softly, "but that was a great shot."

Nicole grinned. "You play?"

Eddie nodded.

Nicole tossed him the ball. "Let's see how good."

Although Eddie was thin and not very tall, he was an agile player. By the time they were finished, the three had become friends.

Anyone who can play ball like that, Matthew thought, has to be a good guy.

Even though basketball season was over, Matthew invited Eddie to shoot hoops with his friends from the team, so they could stay in shape. Eddie had joined them on Matthew's driveway almost every day for the last week. Everyone was having a good time.

Matthew wished the good times were still going on. He shook the memory from his head. "It gets worse," Matthew said to Nicole and Jenna.

"Worse?"

"Yeah."

"No . . . you didn't do the same thing?"

Matthew nodded. "I was busy. I didn't want to miss all the fun . . ."

"I can't believe it," Nicole snapped. "That's demented. Did you turn it in?"

Matthew shook his head. "We just found out before anyone brought it to school."

"Do you realize how lucky you are? Did you ever think about what *could* have happened? First, if the school found out that everyone turned in the same paper, they would figure out really fast that you got it from the internet. Then they would have to punish you. That's plagiarism, Matthew. You could have gotten kicked off the basketball team, suspended from school . . ."

"I know."

"Did you hear about the kid from RCC?" Nicole continued. "He got expelled from community college for plagiarism. He copied stuff from the internet and put it in his paper without citing the author."

"How would anyone find that out?"

"There are websites and software just for that purpose," Nicole said. "They can trace just about anything online." She looked at Jenna. "You're in Mr. Richie's class too?"

Jenna nodded.

"Don't tell me you bought the same paper?"

"No," Jenna frowned. "Even if I wanted to buy it, I don't have enough money. I also read the school newspaper."

Jenna reached into her backpack and pulled out *The Rhodes Reporter*. "See," she grinned meanly, "everyone knows about that kid."

Matthew took the newspaper and read, with Nicole looking over his shoulder.

The Rhodes Reporter

RCC Student Claims He's Innocent

By Kyle Harris, Editor-in-Chief

Chad Norton, a freshman at Rhodes Community College was expelled from school after being found guilty of plagiarism. RCC Dean of Student Discipline stated that "plagiarism is a very serious crime and must be treated accordingly."

Norton was very angry. As a journalism student, he knows all about plagiarism. "Plagiarism is a serious crime," Norton admits, "but I'm not a plagiarist." Norton says he's innocent because all he did was take written words off the internet and put it into his paper. "It's like stealing a stop sign," Norton claims, "the words belong to all of us."

Norton says he will appeal the decision but has little hope that he will win. "The people at RCC just don't understand the internet."

Popularity

By Sofia-Marie Gutilla

A lot of people here at Rhodes Middle School have to "fit in" with the crowd. The Pradas, Kate Spades, etc. seem to be so influential. But all for what? Popularity is so important to some people. Sometimes this can lead to bullying, teasing, and more. But for what? Again, I say that just living your life and being HAPPY and HEALTHY is more important than spending so much money to "fit in" with the crowd.

Help a Little Kid!

By Loretta C. Jacobs

Help a little kid in the neighborhood!
He is two years old and everyone calls him Pepper. Pepper has leukemia. His mother is single and can't afford the treatment for his disease. Pepper's older sister is nine years old. "I just want my brother to live," she told me. I need to find a way to help."

Anyone who would like to sponsor Pepper and help him cure his leukemia, please call the main office.

Congratulations Mike! You deserve to win the Best All-Around Middle School Athlete of the Year.

Rhodes Community Center is Proud of you!

Nicole shook her head. "Chad Norton has no clue what he did." She looked at Jenna. "At least someone has a brain *here*. Just think about it, Matthew. Whoever sold you that paper *knows* who you are; he can blackmail you at any time."

Matthew shuddered.

"Well, at least you were lucky enough to find out before you turned it in."

"Maybe."

"Maybe?"

"How do I know that other kids didn't buy the same paper? I found out about it because someone e-mailed me and said for thirty dollars . . ."

"I got the same e-mail," Jenna said pettishly.

"You were set up," Nicole groaned, "by an e-bully."

"An e-bully?" Jenna asked.

"Electronic bully," Nicole sighed. "You know, they do the same things as a bully on the street except it's all online. Think about it - the e-bully could even be the crazy bus driver. Who knows what he does online? The bottom line is that you were *e-bullied* into believing he had the power."

"I was set up?" Matthew grimaced.

"You lucked out on this one."

"I don't understand."

"*Think*," Nicole sighed. "This e-bully sent you and a bunch of other people - maybe everyone in Mr. Richie's classes - an e-mail to buy this paper. If you all turned it in, everyone would be in big trouble except the kid who sold the paper and the kids that didn't buy it. What a great scam. Once he took your money, the e-bully turned into a real crook. A cybercrook," Nicole chuckled. "Everyone knows that there's a thin line between bullies and criminals."

There was an awkward silence.

"Oh, well," Nicole added. "At least you marked the money so you could track it."

"Marked the money?"

Nicole stared at him contemptuously. "You *did* mark the money?"

"What are you talking about? Only banks and cops could do that."

"Are you telling me," Nicole spoke distinctly, "that you don't know *how* to mark money?"

Matthew just stared at her.

"Where have you been?" Nicole demanded. "Don't tell me you

haven't heard of wheresgeorge.com?"

"Sure I have," Matthew lied.

"You're lying."

"No, I'm not."

"I know when you're lying, Matthew. You can never fool me - or have you forgotten that too?"

"Sure."

"I know all about wheresgeorge.com," Jenna said sweetly.

Nicole grinned. "Everyone but Matthew knows about it."

"Enough! You might as well tell me what . . ."

"It's too late," Nicole taunted him. "If you knew about wheresgeorge.com, you could have marked the bills and tracked where they went."

"I don't understand."

Nicole sighed.

"It's simple," Jenna sat up straight. "You register the serial numbers of all your dollar bills - whether they're ones, fives, or tens - on wheresgeorge.com. Then you mark on the bill a set of instructions to contact wheresgeorge.com. The person who gets the bills can log on and report where and how he received it."

"Give me a break," Matthew groaned. "Do you think a cybercrook would do that?"

"Stupid," Nicole frowned, "you don't mark all the bills. He probably doesn't even notice it at first. He stuffs it into his pocket or wallet or wherever he keeps money. Then suddenly he pulls it out and sees the message - who could resist checking it out?"

"It's anonymous," Jenna added haughtily.

"So what good would that do for me?"

"You might not know his name - but you know the time and place. You would also have the chance to contact him anonymously and search for clues."

"Big deal."

"*Think*, Matthew. You might not get his name, but you could talk to him directly. You never know where something like that will go."

"Yeah, sure," Matthew agreed unwillingly.

"It doesn't matter now anyway. You can't track those bills when you haven't marked them."

"I have a bigger problem than that, right now," Matthew grimaced. "If

I tell the other kids about the paper, they'll all know I tried to buy one on the internet. If I don't tell the other kids, they might have bought the paper too and will get in trouble. Most of the basketball team is in that class. If they get suspended and thrown off the basketball team . . ."

Nicole finished his sentence, "they will never make varsity in 9th grade." She nodded. "You have another problem too."

"What's that?"

"When is the paper due?"

"Friday."

"Well," Nicole frowned, "you have a lot of work to do now, don't you?"

Matthew stared at her while Gizmo buried his head beneath his paws.

"How am I going to write a paper in such a short time?" Matthew asked Nicole. "Jenna - any suggestions?"

Jenna shook her head. "I'm still working on mine."

"Find someone to help you who knows a lot about the subject, or who is a good researcher," Nicole suggested. "Don't ask anyone here - they've got the same paper due. Maybe one of your friends who lives outside the neighborhood?"

Matthew's stomach felt queasy. How was he going to find someone to help write a paper by Friday? He took a deep breath. There was only one place he could go . . . they certainly had the street smarts. Would they be there for him?

Illustration Credit: Jordan Wolfson

Chapter Three
Burnt Beyond Repair

The Tangled Web was Matthew's favorite chat room. His online friends were always there for him. He spoke online with the kids all the time, sharing problems, telling stories, and just having fun.

Matthew logged online.

Welcome to the Tangled Web
Hoops enters the room.

Gigs> Yo Hoops.
Media> How u doing?
Wheels> Hows basketball going?

Matthew's screen name was Hoops. He called himself that because of his last name, Hooper. It seemed natural since playing basketball was such a big part of his life.

Hoops> Hi guys. i have a real problem. Can anyone help me?
Gigs> u always have problems, Hoops.
Hoops> This is big
Wheels> lol it's always a big problem :-)

Media enters the room

Media> Whats doing guys?
Gigs> Hoops has a problem.
Media> Hoops always has problems.
Hoops> Cool it guys. This is 4 real.

Red enters the room.

Red> Hoops has a problem? Great - Hoops problems are so much fun vbg
Hoops> I'm not kidding.
Gigs> Chill out. Whats your problem?

Media> Tell us Hoops.
Hoops> i have 2 write a paper by Friday morning.
Gigs> *All* of us have papers due Friday. That's not a problem.
Hoops> Yeah, it is. You see i had a paper 4 social studies but then i found out that a lot of other people in my class had the same paper.
Media> How did that happen?
Gigs> Be real. He bought it.
Media> u bought a paper? :-(
Hoops> Yeah. Someone sent me an e-mail saying i could buy a paper that was sure 2 get over a 90 in my social studies class.
Wheels> And u bought it? :-0
Hoops> Yeah. It was a good paper.
Gigs> How much did he take u 4?
Hoops> Thirty bucks.
Media> That was really dumb.
Hoops> i know that now. At the time it seemed like a good idea.
Red> i read about online scams all the time. i guess u just became a victim Hoops. Almost everyday there's a new article about internet scams. My favorite is about this 13-year old kid who went on e-bay and bought some crazy stuff like an old sports car convertible, a famous painting, and a complete medical office in Florida. No one knew until a company called from Canada to discuss how they should deliver the antique bed that he bought. The bed belonged to the first Prime Minister of Canada. It had been posted at $12,000 and the kid bid $900,000!
Gigs> rotfl What happened next?
Red> His parents picked up the call from Canada. i heard they took his computer away forever :-)
Wheels> It just shows u can't trust what u buy online.
Media> Unless u know who u r buying it from - like a regular store.
Gigs> Yeah, sure. A kid from my school got one of those papers from an online store. It cost him seven bucks a page.
Hoops> Cheap . . .

Gigs> Not really. He turned in the paper he bought.
Hoops> i don't understand.
Wheels> u really don't get it, Hoops. Those online papers are sold as models. They say all over the sites that plagiarism is against the law. U r supposed 2 buy those papers and use them as a source. They even say u have to list them in the bibliography.
Gigs> Right. If u turn in the paper that u bought, u r going 2 get caught.
Hoops> How?
Gigs> Teachers can always figure that stuff out. They know the websites 2 check. ;-0
Wheels> Teachers *know* to look for those things.
Red> U r really lucky u didn't get caught Hoops.
Media> It seems like it's a lot easier just to do your own work.
Hoops> w/e
Wheels> Yeah, Hoops. Didn't u learn your lesson about how it feels stealing other peoples' stuff?
Media> It takes less time 2 do the paper yourself then 2 figure out how 2 beat the system.
Red> AWGTHTGTTA
Gigs> What does that mean Red?
Red> lol r we going 2 have 2 go through that again?
Gigs> Never heard that one before :-(
Media> Here's the big question, Hoops. Do the other kids know they have the same paper?
Hoops> i don't know.
Wheels> Ok. Now i get it. u have to write a paper by Friday because u think u bought the same paper everyone else did?
Hoops> right
Wheels> u don't know who sold u - or anyone else - that paper?
Media> *that* person knows u and all the kids who bought it?
Gigs> bbr
Red> What does *that* mean, Gigs :-(?
Gigs> lol u think u are the only one who can come up with letters?
Red> Not fair

Gigs> Ok. Burnt beyond repair. Hoops is bbr because he's got to warn the other kids that they all have the same paper AND make sure no one knows he's sounding the warning. If the kid who sold the papers guesses that Hoops is talking, he can do some real damage.

Media> Bad place.

Hoops> How can i do that?

Red> Let's think about it.

Wheels> How about this? Post the warning anonymously where all the kids will c it but won't know it's u.

Red> Where?

Wheels> Someplace everyone checks online.

Hoops> i have an idea. How about the school's online bulletin board?

Wheels> Does everyone read it?

Hoops> Yeah. u never know what's there - like a sighting of a crazy bus driver :-)

Media> How about the school?

Hoops> i don't know.

Media> Be very careful what u say. No one has done anything wrong yet. u don't want to get u or anyone else in trouble for something that never took off.

Hoops> bbr

Media> Not if u r really careful.

Hoops> Yeah right. My friend says everything would have been solved if i tracked the money.

Wheels> How do u track the money? Through wheresgeorge.com?

Hoops> How come u know about it?

Wheels> Everyone knows about wheresgeorge.com

Red> Its an awesome site. Do u know that there r over one million users on wheresgeorge.com?

Gigs> Cool. i heard there's over 90 million dollars worth of marked bills.

Media> omg i never even got one. :-0

Hoops> It adds up 2 only a small percentage of all the money people use everyday in the US.

Red> George bills have turned up in the strangest places all

over the world 2.
Media> Where?
Red> Fortune tellers, charities, casinos, grocery stores, fast food restaurants and all the regular places u can think of. There was even one guy who bought a VCR in dollar bills all marked with the wheresgeorge saying: "see where I've been, track where I go." What difference does it make if u r going 2 spend the money anyway?
Wheels> i heard that one bill traveled from New Jersey 2 Ireland and back. Another guy found a wheresgeorge bill after a California earthquake. He wrote on the website that it survived the earthquake with the courage of a C note.
Gigs> lol i heard there's a whereswilly.com 4 Canadians, 2.
Red> That's true, Gigs.
Wheels> Some guy tried 2 "sell" his services on ebay. He had people bidding on him taking their wheresgeorge bill and circulating them in Nebraska.
Media> Isn't marking money against the law?
Red> Well, sort of. i mean wheresgeorge had the Secret Service after him 4 a while. But the law says that it's only illegal when u mess up a bill so bad it can't be used - u know, tear or shred it, color over it, that kind of thing. People in wheresgeorge WANT their bills 2 be used - they just write little messages on them.
Gigs> It's a game - 2 c how many hits u can get and from how far away. Some people have posted great maps tracking their hits, others compete for the number of bills they put online - all sorts of stuff. Best of all, its free!
Hoops> vbf Enough! i didn't mark the bills so i can't do anything now.
Media> That's a pity
Gigs> Maybe next time.
Hoops> There's never going 2 be a next time.
Gigs> That's what u say now.
Media> Ever hear the saying, nsn -- 'never say never?'
Hoops> i learned my lesson. It won't happen again.
Wheels> Yeah sure, Hoops. We know about u learning lessons. . .

Media> u have bigger problems now. How r u going 2 write that paper?

Matthew had no answer to that question. He didn't respond.

Media> u could do it now.
Hoops> Would of, could of, should of . . . the story of my life.

Before shutting down the computer for the night, Matthew checked the Rhodes Reverie bulletin board.

>Warning!!!!!

Listen up all students from Mr. Richie's eighth grade social studies classes. Someone is scamming ALL OF US online for a lot of money. It can get you in very BIG trouble. Don't waste your $30.

Most of all: **BEWARE!**

The Rhodes Reverie

Tuesday, March 16

Welcome to the Rhodes Middle School online bulletin board. Post your ideas, thoughts, and adventures! Leave messages for friends and talk about your favorite classes!

>Large sum of money missing: $123,761,000. Please return to office.

>Copying off the internet is a mistake not a crime.

>I hate school. Write your name if you do.

>Cow for sale. Brown with white and black spots. Very sweet.

>WANTED - male fugitive on the loose! If found call 1-800-911! Description: two eyes, one nose, one mouth and 2 ears.

Chapter Four
Beware the Ides of March

Matthew hadn't figured *anything* out by Mr. Richie's class on Tuesday.

Mr. Richie put the chalk down with a flourish, turning to face the class. It was the last period of the day. With only three nights left to replace the plagiarized paper, Matthew had to run home after school and get to work. Matthew didn't know how he was ever going to get it done.

No hoops this afternoon, he thought.

Mr. Richie leaned against the desk in the front of the classroom. He paused, scanning the waiting faces.

Mr. Richie was one of the most popular teachers at Rhodes Middle School. He was strong and athletic, with implacable brown eyes and a quick smile. He *understood* what it was like to be a kid in middle school. Best of all, Mr. Richie had his own band. Sometimes he would perform at county fundraisers. The students loved it.

Mr. Richie cleared his throat. "I saw this post on the school's online bulletin board," he began, picking up a paper from his desk. "I don't know if you've seen it so," he glanced at Matthew, "I decided to read it to you."

Matthew squirmed.

You could hear a pin drop in the room.

"It was posted," Mr. Richie continued, "at 10 P.M. on Monday, March 15th. Do you guys know what March 15th is? It's called the *Ides of March*. You might remember it from reading Shakespeare's *Julius Caesar* in English class. The soothsayer or fortuneteller says to Caesar, "*Beware the Ides of March*." That's because Caesar is going to be killed on that day. Caesar ignored the warning. Ever since then, the Ides of March are foreboding just like the post that says *beware*."

He paused. Mike shuffled his feet beneath the desk. Eddie glanced out the window. Matthew stared at his hands.

"Except this 'beware' means something very different." Mr. Richie began to read from the paper. "Listen up all students from Mr. Richie's eighth grade social studies classes." He stopped. "That's you guys," he scowled. "Someone is scamming us online for a lot of money. It can get you in very BIG trouble. Don't waste your $30. Most of all: beware."

Mr. Richie bellowed the word 'beware' so it sounded like a 12-wheeler tractor-trailer rather than his usual friendly voice.

No one spoke.

"I find it very strange."

Mike glared at Eddie. Matthew nonchalantly chewed on his pen.

"Anyone here know what it's about?" Mr. Richie demanded.

There was no response.

"I don't know *what* this post is saying," Mr. Richie sighed. "Obviously, the person who wrote it is trying to tell us something. Thirty dollars is a lot of money. I would imagine it's enough money to buy things you guys would want like a few CDs, a new computer game, or even a paper off the internet. I think you should consider this message very carefully while I intend to obliterate it from my mind. However, if you need me, my door is always open . . ."

Mr. Richie scanned the room.

There were no raised hands.

"OK," Mr. Richie concluded. "I guess there's no discussion *here*. Have a good day, and don't forget that your paper is due on Friday. If you need any last-minute help, now is the time to ask. I don't think I need to remind you that plagiarism is against the law. Adults *and* kids are severely punished when they're caught."

No one looked at Mr. Richie.

"OK," Mr. Richie said sternly. "Go home and finish your papers."

The school day was over.

The classroom quickly filled with the sounds of books closing, papers shuffling, and backpacks being zipped. Usually the kids were noisy, talking about after-school activities, plans for the rest of the day, or walking home together.

No one said a word.

One-by-one the students filed out of the classroom. When Matthew reached the hallway, he noticed that most of the kids had grouped into tight huddles, talking intensely. Dylan, as usual, stood by himself taking it all in. Everyone knew Dylan was the school loner.

Matthew passed by, eavesdropping on their conversations.

"Who put that post on the *Rhodes Reverie*?"

"It had to be the guy selling papers for Mr. Richie's class."

"I think a lot of us bought that *same* paper."

"I bought a paper from an anonymous e-mailer. Did you?"

"My paper is about Machu Picchu. What's your paper on?"

"How much did you pay?"

"Who sold the paper?"

"Where is my money?"

"How am I going to write an entire paper by Friday?"

Matthew wanted to get away from all the questions. He could feel the panic in the air. Suddenly, someone grabbed his shirt and yanked him into a group.

"We know who sold the papers," Mike growled.

Sara stood right next to Mike, her hand across his arm. "You're right, Mike," she cooed.

Sara and Mike had a relationship. They had been together for exactly one month. They hooked up just about the same time that Mr. Richie assigned the paper. Interesting, Matthew thought distractedly. He stared at the gold locket hanging on Sara's neck that Mike had bought her for their four-week anniversary. Matthew thought it was stupid, but Mike was very proud of the tiny picture of himself that he squeezed into the gold charm. Sara wore it everyday.

"Yeah," JC said, interrupting Matthew's thoughts, "Mike told me." JC

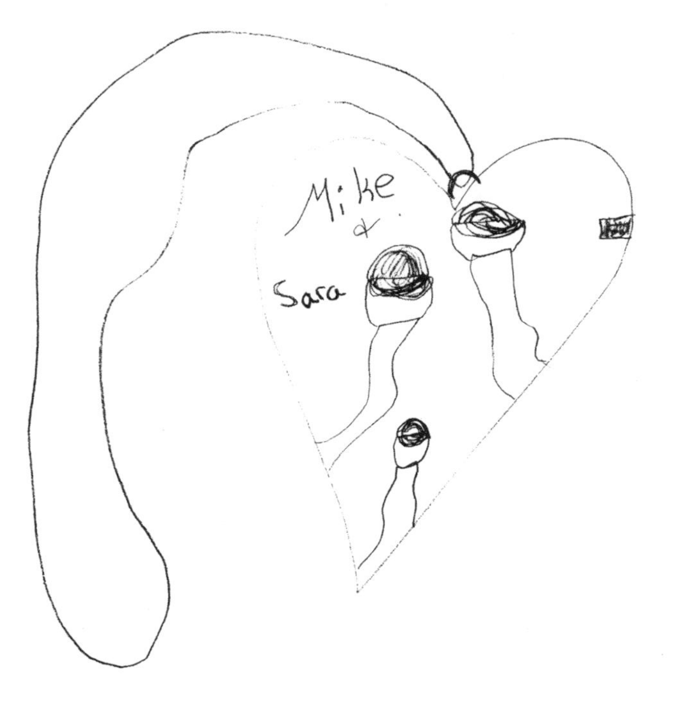

Illustration Credit: Sean Keegan

was Jon Chang Smith, one of the starters on the Rhodes Runners Basketball Team.

"You didn't have to buy a paper," Dan said, one of the best point guards in the league. Dan was a computer genius who got top grades in all his classes. "No one made you do it."

"Look who's talking," Mike grumbled, "you don't *need* to buy a paper."

"Cool it," Matthew said. "That's not the point."

"What is the point?" JC asked.

"Yeah," Robby said. "What is the point?" Even though Robby wasn't on the basketball team there was a strong camaraderie between him and the players. Robby was the sports photographer for *The Rhodes Reporter*, the middle school newspaper. He spent a lot of time with Kyle at school games.

"Someone scammed us," Mike growled, "and I know who."

"Yeah, Mike, someone scammed us." Kyle echoed him. Kyle always followed Mike. Kyle was short, skinny, and nerdy with no athletic ability. He was really smart, though, and did a great job as the Editor-in-Chief of the school newspaper. Mike allowed him to tag along on many team outings. Many of Kyle's stories featured Mike in one sport or another. The girls *loved* Kyle's articles about Mike. They cut out and pasted them, along with Robby's photos, inside their lockers and notebooks, talking excitedly about Mike and forgetting who actually wrote the articles.

"Who?" Eddie asked, standing behind Matthew. "Who would do something like that?"

Matthew, JC, and Dan were silent. Alyssa, Breanna, and Jenna moved closer to hear Mike's response. Breanna stared longingly, never noticing that Kyle was watching her every move. Sara narrowed her eyes, contemptuously watching Breanna.

"It's so simple even a sixth grader could figure it out," Mike ventured.

"What do you mean?" Eddie's voice was subdued.

"You're Latino, you wrote the paper - you picked the subject 'cause you know all about that stuff," Mike's voice began to rise.

"What do you mean?" There was fear in Eddie's eyes.

"Who ever heard of Machu Picchu before that paper? Only someone from *there*," Mike retorted.

"What do you mean - from *there*?" Eddie stepped back.

The crowd around them grew larger.

Kyle pulled his tiny black tape recorder from his pocket. Kyle *always* carried his tape recorder just in case he came across a good story for *The Rhodes Reporter*. He came from a family of writers - his dad was a computer technical writer and his uncle an advertising copywriter. Kyle told everyone that when he grew up, he was going to become a famous journalist.

Kyle thrust the tape recorder in front of Mike's face. Mike frowned, but didn't try to push it away.

"You wrote the paper," Mike sneered at Eddie, "then sold it to all of us. You made a whole lot of money scamming us, didn't you, Pizarro? Just like those Spanish guys who stole the gold and burned all the villages in their path. You burned *us*. Then you stuck that post online so no one would turn in the paper and get into trouble. You thought no one would be smart enough to figure it out. If it wasn't for that demented dog Matthew is puppy-sitting, you would have gotten away with it."

Eddie raised his voice. "Liar," he said futilely.

Mike handed his books to Sara and flexed his biceps. "Thief," he roared. "I'll flatten you in a minute."

Eddie stared at him, his eyes filled with uncertainty. "I don't fight," he said so softly that most of the kids couldn't hear him.

The crowd gave them more space.

"Eddie did it?" Matthew heard someone say.

"Eddie Pizarro scammed us?"

"What do you expect from his . . . kind?"

"They're all thieves anyway . . ."

"Wait," Matthew tried to sound intimidating. He stepped between Mike and Eddie. Matthew knew how it felt to have everyone turn against you. It had happened to him before, and he was determined not to blame Eddie unless they were absolutely sure he was guilty. At the same time, Matthew was afraid Mike would turn against him. Matthew just wanted to stop everything from moving forward. "We don't know anything yet."

"Yeah, Hooper? We know a lot," Mike shoved Matthew. "We know that Eddie wrote the paper. We know that he's Latino and gets all that stuff. We know that he has a 98 in Spanish class and that his father has been in jail like the rest of them."

"Like the rest of them?" Matthew asked, surprised.

"My father has never been in jail," Eddie edged away. Matthew was caught in the middle.

"All your people end up in jail," Mike harassed him.

"Mike, don't," Matthew pleaded, trying to hold him back. Matthew had seen Mike get angry before, bullying kids until they were in tears. That's why no one ever challenged Mike. Everyone was afraid of becoming Mike's victim.

Eddie's voice was barely audible. "I don't fight lowlifes like you."

Mike raised his fists and began stalking Eddie like a wrestler in a ring. Eddie, with his arms flapping at his side, watched Mike helplessly.

Suddenly, Mr. Richie appeared.

"What's going on here?" He yelled above the kids.

They backed away.

Matthew, Eddie, and Mike stared at him sheepishly.

"I should take the three of you down to the principal's office," Mr. Richie said harshly. "Why are you fighting in the hall?"

Matthew began to say something. Instead, he quickly closed his mouth.

Eddie looked off in the distance. "I'm not fighting," he said softly. Once again, no one heard him.

Mike stared at his fists.

"You guys know better," Mr. Richie continued. "What was this all about?"

No one would speak.

"Out of here," Mr. Richie waved away the crowd. The kids scattered. "The three of you - you're lucky you didn't get started. You know the rules about fighting on school property. You play this stuff out on the court with a ball, not with your fists."

Matthew glared at Mike and Eddie. How did he get in the middle of this mess?

"Pick up your books and get out of here," Mr. Richie added. "I better not hear about any more fights on or off school property. If I do . . . well, you know what's going to happen."

The three boys nodded.

"Get out!" Mr. Richie demanded.

Get out! Get out! Matthew felt sick.

Run. Run. Find a safe spot.

The words ran through Matthew's mind. He ran and ran, trying to drive the frustration out of his body. Before he knew it, he found himself home staring into his computer screen.

Maybe someone out there was available to rescue him from his own tangled trails?

Chapter Five
Friend or Fraud?

Welcome to the Tangled Web
Hoops enters the room.

Gigs> Yo Hoops.
Media> How u doing?
Wheels> Hows the problem?
Hoops> [breathlessly] i almost got into a fight today trying to keep the guys from duking it out.
Gigs> What do u mean? :-(
Hoops> Mike wanted 2 fight because he wants his money back. Eddie is scared.
Media> Eddie is smart.
Hoops> Maybe 2 smart. Maybe Eddie *did* sell the papers.
Media> Y?

Matthew recalled Eddie's words when he first discovered that Mike's paper was the same as his.

I don't believe this is happening. How did he get my paper?
Were those the words of a guilty man?

Hoops> i just don't know.
Media> Btw, don't u have a bigger problem than that, Hoops?
Hoops> Whats that?

Media> It doesn't matter whether or not Eddie sold the paper. u need something 4 Friday.
Hoops> [sigh] i know.
Wheels> What are u going 2 do?
Hoops> How can i write a new paper?
Gigs> Its going 2 be a long couple of days Hoops.
Media> Get to work. Whats your subject?
Hoops> South America.
Media> What was the paper u bought about?

Hoops> Machu Picchu.
Media> Interesting.
Hoops> Why?
Media> Well Machu Picchu is all about being lost and found. Kind of like u. Lost a paper and now u have 2 find 1.
Hoops> So?
Media> Here's what u do. Find some online research about Machu Picchu. u already know something about it if u read the paper u bought. Go 2 places u can trust - like websites that have an .edu at the end. It usually means that they're educational - schools or colleges - and u can count on what they say.
Wheels> Rite. Newspapers are a good place 2 do online research 2. Make sure u go to the best ones like NYTimes.com and Newsday.com
Red> i like online encyclopedias like Encarta.com where they have lots of pictures.
Gigs> There's great site on The Rams Page - just check out Bellmore-Merrick CHSD and click on Merrick Avenue Middle School. It gets u a lot of places.
Media> It takes a long time but u can do it Hoops. Get organized. The best way to start is check out the search engines.
Wheels> Try the metasearch engines. They get u more stuff.
Hoops> Whats a metasearch engine?
Wheels> A search engine goes through the internet 2 find websites about your subject. No single search engine has all the sites listed. A metasearch engine searches other search engines, takes out any duplicates, and then ranks your results.
Red> Like an index of indexes.
Wheels> Something like that.
Hoops> tnx i wish there was a search engine to help me figure out who sold the papers.
Red> 2 easy
Media> Write the paper and then worry about it.
Red> Why don't u go 2 Ask Jeeves at ajkids.com and type in a question like why does Matthew come up with so many problems lol

Hoops> can i ask jeeves who the cybercrook is?
Gigs> lol
Hoops> Then what?
Media> Get to work! And don't plagiarize.
Hoops> What about the cybercrook, Eddie, Mike and fighting and . . .
Media> Cool it. Once the papers are done everyone will calm down.
Hoops> I'm not so sure.
Gigs> I'm not sure either Hoops. That Mike guy sounds like a real bully. And bullies love to show how strong they r.
Media> i hope u r wrong Gigs.
Gigs> i hope so 2. i have a feeling that this isn't the end of the story.
Media> This isn't a story, it's real life.
Gigs> Yeah. g2g
Media> bbl
Red> b4n
Wheels> c u
Hoops> tnx bbl

Matthew had to think everything through very carefully. He took a deep breath.

Suddenly Gizmo barked. Someone must have rung the doorbell.

Downstairs, Mom opened the door. Matthew could hear voices but not identify who was speaking. Mom finally called up to him.

"Eddie is here to see you."

"Coming," Matthew said and pushed his chair away from the computer. What could Eddie possibly have to say to him at this time?

Eddie stood in the foyer, shifting his weight back and forth from one foot to the other. He was wearing a dark-colored t-shirt and washed out jeans. Although it was cool outside, Eddie was sweating.

"Yo," Matthew said.

Eddie looked up and nodded.

Mom smiled. "I'll go back to my work," she said, leaving them alone.

There was a long silence. Matthew was determined not to be the first one to speak.

Eddie rubbed his hands together. "I want to talk," he said finally.

"Yeah," Matthew mumbled.

"I mean I really want to talk."

Matthew shook his head.

"I want you to understand . . . no," Eddie paused. "Let me start again. I just don't know exactly how to say this so I'll say it straight. I'm new to the school, and I guess no one really knows me. The first person I met here was Dylan, and he gave me the cold shoulder."

"Why?"

Eddie took a deep breath. "Dylan worked at the **Blitz** before me. Dylan was a real slacker, and the boss hated him. When I started working there, the boss cut Dylan's hours. Dylan got ticked off and quit. He blamed it all on me."

Matthew didn't know what to say. "We all know Dylan is weird but harmless."

Eddie nodded. "I guess. All I know is that you've been trying to be a friend to me, and I really appreciate it."

Matthew was wary.

"I don't feel like I owe an explanation to *anyone*," Eddie said defiantly. "I'm here because I choose to be, not because I have to."

"Understood."

Eddie diverted his eyes, taking a few steps away from Matthew. It was apparent that Eddie was embarrassed and found it very difficult to speak.

"I'm not used to talking like this," Eddie said softly, staring at the floor. "I mean, this kind of stuff is . . . stupid. Know what I mean?"

Matthew didn't know exactly what Eddie meant, but he nodded anyway.

"Ok," Eddie took a deep breath. "Here goes. I . . . I just want to tell you that I'm turning in my Machu Picchu paper. I wrote it, man. I have a *right* to turn it in. I don't know how you or Mike or anyone else got it. All I know is that I wanted it to be good - really good - so I had Mr. Richie approve the first draft, right off the floppy disk. Mr. Richie and I both *know* who wrote it."

Matthew wondered why Eddie was trying so hard to justify himself.

"So I'm turning it in," Eddie concluded.

"Did you *listen* to Mr. Richie?"

"No. Yes. It doesn't matter. I wrote the paper, and I should be able to turn it in."

"OK," Matthew sighed. "It's your life."

"Yeah," Eddie said, his voice quivering.

There was an awkward silence.

"Uh . . . do you want to hang out?" Eddie asked finally.

"*I* have a paper to write," Matthew retorted.

"You believe him, don't you?"

"Who?"

"Mike."

"I don't know what to believe."

"I thought you were my friend. Can you imagine what it feels like to be accused of something you didn't do? Just because your last name is Pizarro?"

Once again Matthew remembered Eddie's words when he saw the paper.

I don't believe this is happening. How did he get my paper?

It was his first, unedited reaction.

"This has nothing to do with your name," Matthew said softly.

Eddie's shoulders slumped. "Yeah, that's what you think. That's what everyone thinks who doesn't have something different about them - darker skin, differently-shaped eyes, an unpopular religion - you name it. You always think it can never be that. Well think again, man. It can and is that. If you slip up, people give you a second chance. If I slip up . . . well, people like Mike just say, *what do you expect of a Hispanic?*"

"That's not true."

"Let me tell you something," Eddie continued, ignoring Matthew's protest. "I was born here; so was my mom. Her parents, my dad, and his parents came from a country called El Salvador, in Central America. Central America is not the same as South America. They came north with Dad in the early '80s because there was a civil war going on; they were afraid the army would kidnap Dad and force him into becoming a soldier. Can you imagine being afraid to walk down your block because someone might stick a gun in your back and make you fight a war and *kill* people?"

Matthew stared at Eddie, wide-eyed. He had a nauseating feeling in the pit of his stomach.

"When he got to this country, Dad had to go back to school. He was a student of Spanish Literature at the university in El Salvador, but here he was nothing. He had to work really hard to learn English and study for years before he could get a job as a professor at Rhodes. Along the way he met Mom and well . . ." Eddie smiled. "We live in faculty housing so I can go to Rhodes Middle School. My parents work *hard*, Matthew. Do you think I would disappoint them by selling some stupid papers?"

Matthew didn't know what to say or think.

"Mike is telling everyone I'm a cybercrook, and it's no surprise because I'm Hispanic." Eddie laughed bitterly. "My dad is a *hero*, Matthew. Because our name is Pizarro, everyone believes that we're worthless."

"Just ignore Mike," Matthew said weakly. "He'll get over it."

"That's not what this is about."

"Really, man," Matthew persisted. "It has nothing to do with your name. Mike is mad because he got caught."

"Yeah, sure. Mike seems to think that I have the inside scoop on Machu Picchu. It should be *easier* for a cybercrook like me . . . easier for someone with the name of Pizarro to write a paper on South America than somebody with the name of Hooper."

"Mike was just mad," Matthew repeated. "He made this dumb connection and ran with the ball. Now he has to write a paper and, you know, Mike's not the greatest student."

"That's not my fault," Eddie scowled. "He shouldn't be bullying me because he got messed up in a scam. It was his choice to take the risk - he took a shortcut and got caught."

"Give him time," Matthew said patiently, "he'll cool off."

"Yeah, after he's got the whole school turned against me. Look at what Sara is saying."

"What would you expect? They're a *couple*."

Eddie shrugged. "And Breanna?"

"She likes Mike too."

"Listen," Eddie added, "I only came here to tell you I'm turning in my paper. You better write your own."

Matthew lunged at the opportunity to change the subject. "That's a problem. I'm having a tough time finding stuff to write about."

Eddie's face softened. "What's your subject?"

"I thought I would stick to Machu Picchu. At least I have a start."

Eddie grinned. "I guess so."

"I just don't know where to go with it."

Eddie rubbed his forehead. "Well, you know what Machu Picchu is about. It was a sacred city built in the clouds -- an Incan place high up in the Andes. After the Spanish Conquistador invaders arrived in South America and then through centuries of terrible rulers, no one remembered Machu Picchu. It was kept secret and finally forgotten. By the time they discovered it, Machu Picchu was old, valuable and untouched."

"I know," Matthew mumbled, "that's what you wrote about."

"Yeah," Eddie said thoughtfully. "You know, when I was doing all my research, I saw a lot of stuff about the guy who discovered it. He was some archeologist from Yale. What was most interesting is that he looked and wore the same hat as Indiana Jones."

"No kidding?"

"Yeah. I didn't write much about him because my paper was long enough. But maybe you could . . ."

Matthew's eyes lit up. "It would make a great paper. *How* Machu Picchu was discovered."

"Right," Eddie grinned.

"Will you help me?" Matthew asked.

Eddie nodded. "I just want to say one thing. You were the first one in Rhodes to ask me to play ball. I owe you one. Yeah, Matthew, I'll help you. That's what friends are for."

"Thanks."

"C'mon," Eddie said, "I'll show you some websites that tell all about him. The guy's name was Hiram Bingham, and you could write ten papers based on stuff you get online. Even," Eddie chuckled, "with a name like Hooper."

The Rhodes Reverie

Wednesday, March 17

Welcome to the Rhodes Middle School online bulletin board. Post your ideas, thoughts, and adventures! Leave messages for friends and talk about your favorite classes!

>Lost black purse - contains a book called MATTHEW'S WEB, calculator, mirror, pens and pencils

>What's the big deal? We all lift stuff online.

>Lost diary - personal information! DO NOT READ IF FOUND!

>GOLDFISH 4 SALE! 99 cents! Fido is a great swimmer and an excellent companion! Have a snake? Feed it Fido!

>Why do the cafeteria chicken nuggets taste like rubber?

Chapter Six
Pointing Fingers

The kids were getting really ticked off.

It was Wednesday, and the paper was due in two days. Everyone in school was talking about it. Matthew saw and heard angry voices all around him from the very beginning of the day.

In first period English they broke into small groups to discuss the book *House of Stairs*. Instead of talking about Lola and Peter, the best characters in the book, the kids whispered about the paper.

Sara was angry, her blonde ponytail bouncing all over her back as she hissed to the group. "I was supposed to go shopping," she frowned, "but now I have to write a paper in two days."

"You mean *you* bought the fake paper too?" Jenna asked, narrowing her green eyes.

"It wasn't fake," Sara retorted, "it was a scam." She played with the locket around her neck. Breanna watched intently as Sara snapped it opened and closed.

"What's the difference?" Matthew demanded.

"What do you know?" Breanna asked sharply.

"Don't be stupid," Sara ventured a guess. "He must have bought it too."

Matthew nodded his head.

"That means," Sara pulled at her ponytail, "that the cybercrook made $120 just from us."

"Not me," Jenna frowned. "Do you think I would waste $30 on a paper I could write myself?"

"You're always complaining about money," Sara retorted.

"You would too," Jenna whispered, "if your dad was unemployed."

"Your dad is unemployed?" Breanna asked.

Jenna stared into the distance. "He was a computer technical consultant," she explained, "working out of an office in the World Trade Center. He got out of the building on September 11 - but his company went out of business a few weeks later. Now he's unemployed."

They were silent.

"I hate terrorists," Jenna added angrily.

"Things will get better," Matthew whispered.

"I have to work really hard," Jenna was rankled, "because we don't even have enough money to live on. Mom's salary just doesn't cut it." She laughed bitterly. "Buying a paper for Mr. Richie's class is definitely out."

No one could find any words. Sara stared at her red fingernails. Breanna chewed on her pen. Matthew recalled what happened with Jenna only a few months ago. JC was the small forward starter on the basketball team. JC really liked Jenna. He asked her to go with him to the **Burger Blitz** on Merrick Road after the Grand Avenue game, one of the biggest events of the season. Jenna told him her parents wouldn't let her go out with him because he's Chinese. Her parents said she should date someone like Matthew or Mike. JC was really upset. Not only was he born in this country, but so were his parents and grandparents. It sounded oddly familiar.

The boys didn't know what to say to JC at the time, so they said nothing.

Matthew wondered if Jenna's father would work for someone who was

Chinese *now* that he lost his job.

"Well," Sara spoke softly, breaking the tension, "that means the cybercrook got only $90 from this group. It's still a lot of money."

"That's just us," Breanna twirled her brown hair around her index finger. "What about the others?"

"Well," Sara fingered her locket, "let's figure it out. There are about thirty to thirty-five kids in each of Mr. Richie's classes. He has four eighth-grade social studies classes - or about," she paused, multiplying the numbers in her head, "130 kids. If each kid paid $30 . . ."

Jenna was the quickest in math. "That's almost $3,900."

Sara gasped, Breanna's eyes widened, and Jenna shook her head.

"Only if *all* the kids bought the paper," Matthew grimaced. He couldn't help *thinking* about all that money. If Eddie was guilty, he was a pretty rich kid by now. Matthew shrugged. What if *he* had done it - and collected all that money? What would he be doing now?

"Even if *half* the kids bought papers, it's still $1,950." Sara nibbled on a fingernail.

"Can you imagine," Jenna murmured, "how much I could help my family with all that money?"

"I could re-do my room," Breanna winced.

"I could buy gold bracelets and chains for the rest of my life," Sara smiled dreamily.

"I could get a new computer," Matthew added. So could Eddie, he thought.

"Yeah, right," Sara shook her ponytail. "The only thing we can get right now is a zero for not turning in our papers."

"Don't think about anything else due for the next two days but writing that stupid paper," Breanna added.

"Minus thirty dollars," Sara scowled.

"We're stuck," Breanna grumbled. "Write the paper in two days or fail."

"It's not that hard," Matthew offered cheerfully.

Sara frowned. "Who do you know?"

Matthew said nothing.

"Maybe it's not hard for you," Breanna moaned, "but I *counted* on that paper. It's just not fair that he did this to us."

"Yeah, right. He fixed all of us." Sara scowled. No one actually said Eddie's name.

Jenna was quiet.

"You think *he* has all the money?" Sara asked.

"Who else?" Breanna muttered.

They stared at Matthew. "What do *you* think?" Sara's voice was suspicious. "After all, isn't he your friend?"

Matthew looked at the three girls. Their eyes were accusing.

"Maybe he didn't do it? Maybe it was someone who stole the paper from him?" Matthew said weakly.

"Like who?" Jenna insisted.

"Maybe . . ." Matthew thought quickly. "Maybe it was the crazy bus driver who aimed for Gizmo on Monday. Yeah, it could definitely be him."

"You can never rule *him* out of anything," Jenna grinned. "After all, today is Wednesday."

"What are you talking about?" Breanna asked.

Sara shook her head. "Let's be real. The crazy bus driver doesn't know how to read stop signs. How could he ever sell papers on the internet? Anyway, what would you expect Matthew to think about Eddie?" She gazed knowingly at the other girls.

"Mike must be right," Breanna said sweetly.

"What do you know?" Sara snapped.

Matthew stared at the three girls.

"You're stupid," Sara snarled, "everyone knows that. You get really awful grades."

Breanna's lower lip trembled slightly.

"No one wants to hang out with you," Sara added, "especially Mike."

"Mike likes me," Breanna said weakly.

Sara laughed loudly. "No one likes you but Kyle, and we all know what a wuss he is. Everyone else just tolerates you. Mike *belongs* to me."

"That's not fair."

"Of course, it's fair. Alyssa told me that all your clothes are hand-me-downs. That's why you always look so bad."

"I don't look so bad."

"Everyone laughs at you behind your back," Sara hissed, "you just don't know about it."

"They don't."

"They do. *Especially* Mike."

Jenna and Matthew glanced at one another. They didn't know what to say.

Breanna's eyes filled with tears. "Alyssa *likes* me. She doesn't laugh behind my back."

"That's what you think."

Breanna turned to Matthew and Jenna. "Do *you* pick on me when I'm not around?"

Jenna glared at Sara.

Matthew couldn't think of anything to say. "We have to work on *House of Stairs*," he suggested.

The three girls eyed him.

"You don't get it, do you?" Sara frowned.

"Get what?"

Sara shook her head. "Yeah, you're right. We have to work on the book, not on Breanna's pitiful social life."

Breanna spread her hands over her face, trying to hide the tears.

"You made her *cry*," Matthew whispered incredulously.

"You just don't get it," Sara said again.

"But you made her cry," he persisted.

"Yeah," Sara smiled, "she'll get over it."

After English class, Matthew grabbed his backpack and walked thoughtfully into the hallway. He was still astounded by the way Sara had treated Breanna. In some ways it was actually *worse* than what Mike was doing to Eddie. *Why do people have to be so mean to one another*, Matthew asked silently? Why can't they just get along? He knew people had been asking that same question since the cavemen. No one had come up with an answer so Matthew decided that it was unlikely he would find the solution.

Suddenly, someone tapped him on the back. Matthew jumped. He had almost forgotten where he was.

"Matthew," Sara said sweetly, twirling the end of her ponytail around her index finger.

"Hi Sara," he responded.

"Going to Spanish?"

"How did you know?"

"I have a class next door to you."

Matthew nodded.

"I'll walk with you?"

Matthew stared at her in disbelief. Sara never wanted to walk with him anywhere.

"How's Mike?" she asked flippantly.

Matthew's eyes narrowed. "Fine."

All the kids knew that Sara bragged about being Mike's girlfriend. Mike loved *that* - but he still talked about other girls. It was simple - there were so many girls who liked Mike's ripped body and tough way of handling people that he had his choice. That was another question Matthew couldn't answer - why did everyone *like* the school bully? For a moment Matthew wondered if the kids really liked Mike or just went along with him because it was easier?

Sara interrupted his thoughts. "Be careful around Breanna."

"What?"

"Be careful around Breanna," Sara repeated. "I know stuff about her so . . ." She hesitated.

"What kind of stuff?"

"I don't like to talk about people."

"You already started."

Sara sighed, "well if you really want to know."

Matthew was curious. "I really want to know."

"You can't tell anyone."

"I won't."

"Breanna comes from a terrible family." Sara sidled up to Matthew and lowered her voice. "Her older sister was caught *stealing*. Breanna and her sister are very close and . . ." Sara shook her head. "Well, look at it this way. Whoever gets involved with Breanna is headed for trouble. Her sister hangs out with this really sketchy group, and if Breanna gets mad, she can get them after us . . ."

"Why are you telling me this?"

"I want to make sure you're safe," Sara frowned. "Annnnnnd," she stretched the word out rhythmically as if singing it in chorus, "I wouldn't be surprised if Breanna was the one who sold those papers."

"Breanna?" Matthew gasped.

"Breanna," Sara said firmly. "She needs the money and with her sister would know exactly what to do and . . ."

The bell rang.

"I'm going to be late . . ." Matthew said quickly.

" . . . and I think she might be *like* Eddie."

"What do you mean?"

Sara smiled knowingly and disappeared into her classroom.

Breanna? Matthew shook his head. He couldn't imagine that the girl who cried because Sara said no one liked her, would be capable of stealing so much money from her classmates -- even if her sister was a thief.

Anything seemed possible - the rest of the day had to get better.

Chapter Seven
Matthew-in-the-Middle

Mrs. Lash's Spanish class was all downhill. It was going well until Alyssa started to talk just like Mike and Sara. No one argued with Alyssa either.

Mrs. Lash was talking about how the European-Spanish people conquered South America and bullied the Indians into converting and adopting western ways. Many countries remained poor and in constant conflict so people moved to the richer United States.

"In this country," Mrs. Lash observed, "*Hispanics* are people, or people who come from families that originally spoke Spanish as a first language."

Then it was Kyle's turn to do his oral report. He brought in a poster presentation for the class. It was a large white board with strange-looking graphs drawn in all different colors. He turned on his tiny black tape recorder and put it on Mrs. Lash's desk. Kyle even liked to record himself.

"The Hispanic population is growing like crazy," Kyle began. "They're the fastest-growing minority group in the US, making up about 13 percent of the entire population." He pointed to a red graph in the center of the poster.

The class listened intently.

"Soon," Kyle continued, "one out of every four students in U.S. public schools will be Hispanic."

"Yeah," Dylan muttered, "and they're all here for our jobs."

"You're right," Kyle whispered angrily. "Some Latinos think they know about writing in English, too."

"You got it right," Dyan muttered

"They have no business trying to teach us how to write English."

"That's enough," Mrs. Lash said sternly.

There was an awkward silence in the classroom. The kids looked around as if they were counting how many Hispanics were sitting behind desks.

Alyssa Harris sat next to Matthew. "Wouldn't you think," she whispered loud enough for everyone to hear, "that one Eddie is enough?"

Matthew couldn't believe what was happening. Sure, Eddie was Hispanic. So? More important, he was a good basketball player. Isn't that what counted? He thought about Mike's words to Eddie.

You're Latino, you wrote the paper - you picked the subject 'cause you know all about that stuff . . . You made a whole lot of money scamming us, didn't you, Pizarro? Just like those Spanish guys who stole the gold and burned all the villages in their path. You burned us.

Matthew shook his head. It sounded archaic as if they were living a hundred years ago when people openly discriminated against Afro-Americans. He remembered seeing a movie about the Civil Rights movement, and how some people hated others just because they had darker skin. He shivered. Was that happening right here in Rhodes? How could it be possible that people accused and hated Eddie just because he was Hispanic?

It simply didn't make any sense. This was Rhodes Middle School, not some pitiful place where narrow-mindedness ruled. People just didn't think like that in his hometown.

Everything looked very different at lunchtime.

The scene made chills run down Matthew's back.

Matthew was late and by the time he walked into the lunchroom it was filled with kids already eating. It was pizza day and the smell of cheese wafted through the room, pierced by the sticky-sweet compliment of peanut butter and jelly. The noise was deafening - kids shouting at each other, food tossed from one end of the table to another amid loud cheers, games played on the slippery surface of the table - Matthew could hardly hear himself think.

All last week Eddie had been eating lunch with Matthew, Mike, JC, and some of the kids from the basketball team. This time, the guys were at their regular table, but Eddie was sitting by himself in a far corner. Eddie's table was completely empty. A few kids turned, glared at Eddie, and then went back to their friends. Matthew shuddered. It all happened so quickly. How could everyone be convinced that Eddie was the cybercrook after only three days? Who had told Eddie to eat alone? Did Eddie feel he could no longer have lunch with the guys?

Matthew knew, too well, what that felt like. It was only a few months since the time that everyone in school believed he had done something very wrong. He was innocent, but the kids were very quick to blame him.

Even his best friends, the guys from the Rhodes Runners basketball team, had shunned him just like they were doing to Eddie. However, when the kids turned away from Matthew, they believed he had done something very wrong. Were they shunning Eddie because he was Hispanic or because Mike had accused him of being the cybercrook? The most insidious question was whether or not Mike accused Eddie because he was Hispanic. Matthew hesitated, trying to figure out what to think and do. Once again, Eddie's words came back to him.

I don't believe this is happening. How did he get my paper?

Matthew thought about how Eddie had helped him with his paper last night, showing him all the websites about Hiram Bingham, the *Indiana Jones*-style archeologist who had discovered Machu Picchu. Was that the work of a guilty kid? He thought about what Eddie had said.

You were the first one in Rhodes to ask me to play ball. I owe you one. Yeah, Matthew, I'll help you. That's what friends are for.

Matthew took a deep breath. He wasn't sure that Eddie was innocent, but he wasn't sure that he was guilty, either. Matthew made his decision.

He went through the food line, bought his pizza, and walked quickly past the guys, headed directly to Eddie's table. Eddie glanced up and saw him. Eddie smiled, nodding appreciatively until Mike grabbed Matthew's shirt. Even from the other side of the cafeteria, Matthew could see Eddie's face fall, the smile droop quickly into a frown.

"Where you going?" Mike asked.

Matthew glanced at the table, filled with his friends.

"I . . ."

Mike didn't allow him to finish. "You're a Rhodes Runner, right?" he demanded.

"Right."

"Then you stick with us."

"I want . . ." Matthew began.

"You stick with *us*," Mike's voice was threatening. "If you know what's good for you."

Matthew stared into Mike's eyes. The anger simmered close to the surface. He looked at the table. JC was concentrating on his pizza. Dan shook his head slowly, as if to say *why start?* Sara and Alyssa picked at their food, Shawn turned away, and tall, lanky Damian grinned. Breanna and Kyle concentrated on their mustard sandwiches.

"You stick with us," Mike said again, "if you know what's good for you."

Matthew looked back at Mike. He was big, ripped, and fierce. Everyone at Rhodes Middle School knew that the worst situation was to be an enemy of Mike. He could make your life miserable.

Matthew glanced unhappily over Mike's shoulder at Eddie. Eddie had already returned to his pizza. Matthew knew what it felt like to be left out - accused of something you never did. Yet he also knew what it felt like to be Mike's enemy. He took another quick look at Dan, JC, Shawn, and Damian.

It was perfectly clear. They all went along because no one wanted to risk being bullied by Mike.

"Get real," Mike's voice rumbled. "If you hang out with him," Mike tilted his head in Eddie's direction, "we might just think you're guilty, too."

"I'm guilty?" Matthew's throat was suddenly very dry.

"Yeah. You know, maybe you were in on the deal, too."

Matthew was flooded with fear. He pictured Sara, Jenna, and Breanna in English class. *What would you expect Matthew to think? Sara gazed knowingly at the other girls.*

He couldn't bear the idea of being ostracized by the kids again. Yet, Matthew hated himself for what he did next.

He put his tray on the table with the guys and made sure he didn't meet Eddie's eyes.

Chapter Eight
Never Say Never

The day ended, as usual, with Mr. Richie's class. Matthew expected the worst.

"I know you will all be on time with your papers," Mr. Richie said, as if he had no idea of what happened. "I hope none of you encounter any more problems."

Eddie, who loved to participate in the discussions in social studies, was strangely silent. Mr. Richie glanced at him several times but said nothing.

Mr. Richie continued with his lesson on South America. "What most of us don't realize," he said evenly, "is that there are well over 32 million people in the United States that report having a Hispanic origin. Most of them live in the California, Texas, and New York."

He took a deep breath.

"The term Hispanic is a catch-all to describe people who come from many different cultures, ethnic groups, and nations. Most Hispanic people in the United States belong to families that originated in Mexico. After that they come from Central America, South America and the Caribbean. Eleven percent are Puerto Rican and five per cent are Cuban. The differences between the people and culture of a country like Colombia and a country like Mexico are enormous. Yet, we lump Hispanics all together. It's like saying there's no difference between people from England and people from France."

There was an odd tension in the class. No one moved or spoke, their eyes fixed on Mr. Richie.

"Sometimes we put people in categories thinking we can understand them better, but instead, it often ends up discriminating against them." Mr. Richie paused. "You know, it's a form of cultural bullying."

Sara raised her hand. "I don't understand."

Mr. Richie nodded. "You're not the only one. Let's look at it in another way. The only thing that all Hispanics have in common is that they speak Spanish. Do you think that people from the United States, India, and South Africa are all the same? Yet we all speak English."

"We have different accents," Sara said.

"So do people from different Spanish-speaking countries."

There was a long silence. "What do you think about cats?" Mr. Richie asked unexpectedly.

The kids looked confused.

"Cats," he repeated. "Do any of you own a cat?"

"Sure," Mike smiled, "my mother loves her silver tabby."

Mr. Richie nodded.

"I have a Siamese," Alyssa offered.

"My cat is a Persian," Kyle grinned.

"How are they different?" Mr. Richie asked.

"That's an easy question," Alyssa giggled. "*Everyone* knows that Siamese cats are very pretty; they meow a lot, and don't like to go outside. Persians are like balls of fur and tabbies - well, tabbies are just alley cats."

"They look, play, and act differently?"

"Of course."

"But they're all cats?" Mr. Richie persisted.

"Sure," Alyssa agreed.

"So are lions. How about a tiger? Or a leopard? Would you have one of them in your house?"

Alyssa smiled. Kyle laughed.

"See my point?" Mr. Richie asked. "We have the same general name or category for so many different types of cats -- just like Hispanics. We have the same general name for so many different types of people."

Mr. Richie smiled. "Keep in mind that it's natural for people to belong to a group. Groups make it easier to relate to one another, communicate, and support what we need. Especially when you have the same interests. Groups can be small, like families, medium-size like basketball teams, or large like political, religious, and ethnic groups. Groups are a very good thing unless they become cruel, maliciously leave people out, or work together to hurt another person or group. Sometimes people in a group lose their individuality and go along with the crowd, not realizing the ramifications of what they're doing."

Eddie, sitting in the back of the room, shook his head vigorously.

"And sometimes," Mr. Richie added, "groups can be dangerous."

"I don't understand," Alyssa raised her hand. "How can they be dangerous?"

Mr. Richie took a deep breath. "There's something called collective behavior. It comes in a lot of different forms. Collective behaviors are ways of thinking, acting, or feeling, that appear in a group of people. They're usually spontaneous, without any structure. For example, think about what happens when you're in a sports stadium. Maybe you're watching baseball, basketball, football, or hockey. Suddenly a bad call is made against your team. Before you know it, the entire crowd rises shouting obscenities at the referee. Now think about yourself. Whether you agree or not, you're probably standing up shouting, too."

"I did that at a Yankee game," Kyle said. "They called the guy out at home when he was really safe. The crowd went nuts."

"And you?"

"I went nuts, too."

"If you were watching television would you have behaved the same way?"

"No," Kyle grinned sheepishly. "I wouldn't have thrown my hot dog at the field."

The kids laughed.

"Here's how it works," Mr. Richie continued, "you take a group of people who are packed in together. Two major things happen. First, people tend to be more suggestible, more likely to do or believe what the rest of the crowd is doing. The next time you're in a crowd, just look up at the sky. Before you know it, everyone else is looking up too."

"Yeah, I've done that on the street. It really works," JC said.

"That's one feature of a crowd. The next is something all of us have experienced. We lose our identity."

"I can never lose my identity," Mike scowled.

"Yeah?" Mr. Richie challenged him. "Let's go back to that Yankee game. When you're cheering because a grand-slam-home-run was just hit, are you "Mike" or a "Yankee fan"?

Mike shrugged.

"The last thing that happens is perhaps the most dangerous. When you trade in your "self" for the identity of the crowd and become more suggestible, this strange feeling of power emerges. Suddenly you *feel* invincible. That's why there are riots after sports events or court decisions. People go out to protest or celebrate or just watch - it doesn't really matter. They lose themselves in the identity of the crowd, get a feeling of power and then are easily led into dangerous behaviors. In the Old South, they hanged Afro-American people from trees using the "lynching mob" mentality. It didn't matter whether or not they were guilty. The group just wanted them dead. Today people loot stores, attack police, and do all sorts of crazy things."

The class was silent.

"That will never happen to me," Kyle said.

"Or me," Dan agreed.

"Never," Alyssa and Sara said in unison.

"Never," Mr Richie frowned, "*say never*."

When Mr. Richie's class was over, Eddie was the first to leave the room.

Matthew desperately wanted to talk to him. He wanted to explain why he had eaten lunch with the guys instead of sitting with Eddie. He felt that Eddie should understand that Matthew had not made the choice himself.

It had been Mike's decision. Eddie had to know that. Matthew didn't get very far before someone grabbed his arm and wrenched him into a huddle.

Matthew stared at the faces: Mike, JC, Dan, Alyssa, Sara, Breanna, Robby, and Kyle.

"Mr. Richie doesn't get it," Mike grumbled. "Yeah, basketball teams are groups, but they're always *good*."

No one dared to contest Mike.

"Mr. Richie doesn't know what he's talking about," Mike continued, anger seeping into his voice. "We're all in a group that's been scammed by that dirty Hispanic, Eddie."

Matthew wanted to ask him how he was sure Eddie was the one who sent the e-mail, sold the papers, and kept the money. Matthew wanted to tell Mike that this was a free country, and everyone was innocent until proven guilty.

Matthew didn't say a word.

I'm too afraid, Matthew thought, *that Mike would turn on me*.

"This group," Mike commanded, "is taking a break. "We're going over to the **Burger Blitz** on Merrick Road," Mike squeezed Matthew's arm.

Sara sidled up to Mike. "You're sooooo right," she cooed.

Breanna glared at Sara.

"We've got a paper due," JC objected.

"I'm not going to let Eddie stop me from going out after school," Mike growled.

"He works *there* at the **Blitz**," Dan remarked. "Do you really want to go?"

"Of course," Alyssa grinned at Sara.

"What about the paper?" JC asked.

"We'll find the time," Mike responded, dropping Matthew's arm and laying his thick biceps over Sara's shoulder. Sara grinned coyly. "We have to make a statement to *him*."

"Let it be," Matthew pleaded.

"You know," Mike regarded him suspiciously, "the way you defend that *Latino* makes me believe you might be in on this whole scam with him."

"I'm not in on it."

"Then prove it."

"Stop," Kyle grabbed Matthew's arm. "Let's just listen to Mike - he's always right. First we'll go to the **Blitz**, and then we'll go home to do the paper." Kyle slipped his tiny black tape recorder from his pocket, but didn't press the "on" button.

"Yeah," Mike declared. "We're not going to let Eddie and his scam interfere with our fun."

Chapter Nine
Eddie's Scam

The **Burger Blitz** on Merrick Road was a fast food joint, walking distance from Rhodes Middle School. After school the Blitz filled up with kids, downing dozens of skinny hamburgers, mounds of greasy fries, and the thick, rich shakes that made it so popular. Since the **Blitz** was one-of-its-kind, it *felt* like McDonald's but looked like a burger place from the '50s, with photos of old cars, screaming teenagers, and red-checkered, plastic tables. There was always radio music and a lot of noise.

The kids from Mr. Richie's class headed over to the **Blitz** as Matthew ran home. He had to take Gizmo for a walk every day after school. Matthew took his puppy-sitting job seriously. Matthew burst into the house, and Gizmo was waiting patiently. The puppy moved quickly as if he didn't want Matthew to waste any time. Matthew wondered what it would be like if he took Gizmo to the **Blitz**. He could see it in his mind - Gizmo tearing up the place, the guys behind the counter trying to catch him and the kids cheering on the puppy. Matthew laughed out loud; Gizmo looked at him curiously.

"Just a thought, Gizmo," Matthew said.

Matthew was sure that Gizmo grinned.

When Gizmo finished his walk, Matthew took him back to the house. He locked the front door and headed straight for the short cut through the Doyle's backyard. It was the fastest route to the **Blitz**. Buddy, the Doyle's big, affectionate Dalmatian, ran to greet him. Matthew paused, allowing Buddy to sniff. Suddenly a warm, doggy tongue was licking his hand.

"Good boy," Matthew smiled, "gotta go."

Matthew was really enjoying this dog thing.

He reached the street and jogged the rest of the way. Standing in front of the **Blitz**, Matthew could see his friends through the large glass window. They sat in their usual spot - the rear corner where there was a table big enough to seat the whole group. There was Dan, smiling quietly and JC sitting next to him, gulping his favorite, a large, chocolate, thick shake. JC *loved* his shakes. Sometimes Mike teased JC because when he was short on money, JC would get a shake instead of food. Mike always figured out a way to tease people.

Mike sat opposite JC with a *huge* pile of food in front of him, including several burgers, fries, and a shake, Alyssa was on his right, nibbling delicately on a burger and Sara was on his left, leaning against him, and playing with her gold locket. Jenna had nothing. Kyle and Breanna were sharing a large order of fries, dipping them into a thick mound of yellow mustard. Matthew chuckled. He couldn't imagine ruining good fries with mustard.

Matthew waved to his friends as he entered the **Blitz**. He didn't notice Eddie standing quietly behind the counter ringing up orders at the cash register.

"Took you long enough," Mike greeted him.

Matthew ignored him. "I had to walk Gizmo," he said to Jenna.

Jenna frowned. "I wish I had a job like *that*."

"What kind of job?" JC asked.

"Puppy-sitting," Jenna responded. "Matthew actually gets paid for puppy sitting."

"Wuss," Mike taunted.

"I'm getting some food," Matthew refused to respond to Mike. "Anyone want something?"

"Yeah," Mike grumbled, "I need another shake." He glanced at the counter. Matthew followed his gaze and saw Eddie.

Matthew knew there was trouble brewing. "I'll get it for you," he said, "what do you want?"

Mike stood up. "I'll get it *myself*."

Matthew knew the look in Mike's eyes. It was like a fire hungrily searching for more fuel to burn. Matthew had seen it many times, particularly when Mike bullied kids at school.

Matthew shivered.

"You know," Jenna said shooting a knowing glance at Matthew, "maybe I'll get something too."

Matthew nodded. The three tentatively approached the counter.

Mike stared aggressively into Eddie's eyes. Eddie backed up. "Can I help you," Eddie asked nervously.

"Yeah, *Latino*, you can." Mike grinned maliciously. "I want a man-sized order of fries - not like one for wimps like you."

Eddie took a deep breath and opened his mouth to respond.

"I want fries too," Jenna said quickly before Eddie could speak.

"Yeah," Matthew took her cue, "I want a burger, fries, and vanilla shake."

Eddie didn't move. The friction mounted. Matthew's hands curled into tight fists before he realized what was happening. Mike leaned closer to Eddie. The pressure grew between them, until Matthew felt like something was going to explode. He was terrified. What would Mike do next?

Although Jenna was six inches shorter than Eddie and half the weight of Mike, she wedged herself between them.

"Easy," she said very softly.

They didn't hear her.

"Easy," she raised her voice.

Eddie glanced at her. A muscle in Mike's jaw twitched.

"Stay cool," Matthew forced himself to sound steady.

"What?" Mike barked.

Jenna and Matthew looked at one another.

"Get us the food, Eddie," Jenna insisted. "*Pul-lease*."

Eddie's lips were a straight line, his eyes narrowed and waiting.

"Get us the food," Jenna said again. "I'm hungry."

"Me too," Matthew added. "I'm hungry."

There was a long pause.

Slowly, like an animal backing off from its attacker, Eddie moved away from the cash register. His eyes never left Mike.

"Hungry," Jenna whined.

"Yeah, sure," Eddie said. He turned away, preparing their order.

Jenna and Matthew exhaled noisily. Mike didn't move.

"Why don't you go back to the table, Mike?" Jenna asked lightly. "We'll bring your food."

"I'm not going to let any lying Latino get the best of me," Mike snarled.

Matthew wanted desperately to say *something*. There were so many words in his mind.

You're a bully Mike and it's ugly.

Being Hispanic has nothing to do with the scam.

Maybe Eddie isn't guilty at all.

No one really likes you Mike - they're just afraid of you.

Matthew was silent.

Eddie returned with the orders, his face set like a statue. He silently rang up Mike's bill. Mike stared at the fries, not touching them. In a subdued voice, Eddie asked for Mike's money. Mike handed him a five-dollar bill. Eddie entered the numbers in the cash register and the drawer popped open sounding like a television gunshot muffled by a silencer. They all stared at the register drawer. Robotically, Eddie reached in to gather Mike's change.

"Hey, *Latino*," Mike's voice was like a hot-orange flame burning in an ice field. "Why don't you steal money from the cash register and not from me?"

Eddie's hands froze. Matthew stared at them, fascinated. They were rigid, trembling with fury.

"Stay cool," Matthew whispered.

Eddie ignored him. Instead, he took a deep breath that rattled in his chest and glared at Mike. "I didn't steal any money from you or anyone else," he whispered. "I don't want anything to do with your kind."

"What kind is that?" Mike snarled.

"A bullying liar," Eddie said apprehensively.

Mike leaned over the counter, his face inches from Eddie's. "You want to say that again?"

Out of the blue, Jenna once again shoved her way between them. "Chill," she said in a high-pitched voice. "I hate to break this thing up but I'm hungry, and I have to baby-sit in an hour."

Eddie inched away from Mike.

"*Please*," Jenna insisted, "I'm hungry."

She put her hands on Mike's huge chest. Mike looked down at Jenna's fingers. Such tiny hands, Matthew thought, yet they could magically stop Mike from pressing forward.

The four of them were suddenly frozen in time. Matthew could hear the music, kids laughing, and the crumpling of paper cups in the background. He could smell the burgers and fries and hear the cook shouting orders in the back. He knew that everyone from his group was watching to see what would happen. It all blended together like slightly blurred scenery in a movie with a camera focused on their unfolding drama.

Finally Eddie backed away slightly. Mike mirrored him. Amazing, Matthew thought, that Jenna's tiny hands could halt the plot.

"Do you want anything else, Jenna?" Eddie asked hoarsely.

"No, I can only afford fries."

"You're not asking me that question," Mike growled. "I guess a liar doesn't care. You wouldn't want to miss the chance to get some more money from us," Mike grabbed his change and threw it at Eddie. "I just made it easy for you."

Illustration Credit: Loretta C. Jacobs

Eddie froze.

Jenna grabbed the money. "Let's go."

Eddie opened his mouth to say something and then changed his mind.

The moment passed.

The tension eased.

Suddenly, Matthew realized that he had been holding his breath. He exhaled. Carefully, as if he were in a slow-motion movie, Matthew paid for his food and followed Mike and Jenna away from the counter.

Eddie watched silently.

It seemed to take forever to get back to the table. No one was talking. They had been waiting for a fight.

Matthew sat as far away from Mike as possible. He spread out his burger, fries, and shake in front of him. Suddenly, he wasn't hungry at all. He stared at the food until he felt very queasy, as if his stomach was rebelling against everything that was happening.

"Pass me the ketchup," Matthew mumbled, not knowing what else to do. He never really knew exactly how the ketchup squirt bottle got into his hands or why he was so terribly angry with Mike. Ketchup brought back a lot of very painful memories when everyone believed that Matthew had done some terrible things. It was just like Eddie - everyone believed that Eddie had sold the papers and collected all the money.

No one believed Eddie was innocent except maybe Matthew.

Yet Matthew wasn't really *sure* that Eddie was innocent - he just wasn't convinced that he was guilty. Like all the courtroom shows on television, Eddie was innocent until proven guilty. Wasn't that the way it was supposed to work?

"He won," Mike said bitterly. "Eddie scammed us all and got to keep the money."

"He beat us," Sara agreed.

"I heard," Alyssa leaned toward Mike, "that he made five thousand dollars."

"We don't know," Jenna said quickly, "how much the scammer made. It all depends on how many people bought the paper."

"That's not what I heard," Alyssa sipped her soda.

"Does it matter?" Mike grumbled. "He has our money, and we don't have a paper."

"That's why we can't stay here too long," JC suggested.

"We'll stay here as long as we want," Mike raised his voice.

The message was clear. They would stay there as long as *Mike* wanted.

Matthew gripped the ketchup bottle tightly.

"We can't trust that guy," Mike continued. "You know that his father was in jail for stealing or something?"

"Maybe it was murder," Sara said capriciously.

"His father is a professor at Rhodes Community College," Matthew said softly. Mike ignored him.

"I heard that he was caught for stealing in his old neighborhood. *With a gun*. That's why his family had to move," Mike grinned.

"They moved," Matthew raised his voice, "because his father got an apartment in faculty housing."

Mike glared at Matthew. "Why are you defending the cybercrook? If the faculty housing is so good, how come you don't live there? I mean, your mother works there doesn't she?"

"Yes . . . but that doesn't mean . . ."

Mike dismissed him. "Eddie's garbage; I know it for a fact."

Matthew clenched the bottle so tightly that a small stream of ketchup

Illustration Credit: Cesar Gonzalez

began to bubble from the top. He stared at it, mesmerized.

"Stay away from him," Mike ordered the group, "until we can figure out a way to get our money back."

"Please pass the ketchup," Jenna said from the other end of the table. Matthew glanced at her. It was clear that she felt exactly the same as him - wanting to stick up for Eddie but afraid of being on Mike's wrong side.

"We'll show him," Mike raised his fist, "that his kind doesn't belong here in Rhodes - and we're not going to tolerate him stealing."

"Yeah," Kyle agreed weakly.

Dan and JC said nothing.

The ketchup boiled over the side of the squirt bottle, dripping onto Matthew's hand. It looked like blood.

"The ketchup," Jenna insisted.

Matthew jumped. Everyone stared at him, waiting for the next move. He held up the squirt bottle, reached past Mike and handed it to Jenna. She reached over to take it, and suddenly Mike snapped the bottle away, holding it high over his head like a trophy.

"I have an idea," he grinned evilly. Mike cleared a space across the table. In big, blood red letters he wrote:

EDDIE'S SCAM

Sara and Alyssa clapped their hands. Mike triumphantly handed the ketchup to Jenna. Matthew, Kyle, JC, Breanna, and Dan stared at the words.

"Hey Eddie," Mike shouted toward the counter, "we had a spill here. Come and clean it up."

Eddie looked at his boss. "Go," his boss said, "I'll cover the cash register."

Reluctantly, Eddie grabbed some rags and a sponge. He headed toward the table.

"Watch this," Mike whispered.

Kyle yanked out his tiny black tape recorder. It was going to be a great story.

All eyes shifted to Eddie.

Eddie reached the table and leaned over to clean up the mess. Suddenly he saw the message. He froze.

"Got you, Latino," Mike growled. "You'll pay for stealing money from us."

"I never stole any money."

"Yeah, who wrote the paper? Who sold it? You think we're so stupid. We all know you did it because your old man was in jail, and he can't get a decent job."

"My father was never in jail," Eddie battled to find the words, " and he has a great job. He teaches Spanish Literature . . ."

"Yeah, sure," Mike glanced around the table, "and my father is President."

JC, Dan, Kyle, Sara and Alyssa laughed nervously. Jenna was silent, a frozen look on her face. Matthew stared at the ketchup dripping down his own hand.

"I didn't do it," Eddie said desperately. "You have to believe me . . . I would never . . ." He stopped abruptly, his eyes fixed on Matthew's hand. "You wrote that," he asked incredulously.

Matthew tried to hide his hand. "I didn't write that . . . I wouldn't . . ."

"You think he's your buddy?" Mike taunted. "Be real. We all think you're a piece of garbage. You don't *deserve* to go to the same school as us."

Mike attacks people just like Sara, Matthew thought suddenly. He could hear Sara's words after English class.

I wouldn't be surprised if Breanna was the one who sold those papers.

Sara had told Breanna no one liked her . . . just as Mike had said to Eddie. Maybe Sara - no, Matthew mentally shook his head. A girl would never do something like stealing a paper and selling it on the internet.

"Why did you write it?" Eddie asked again, interrupting Matthew's thoughts.

"I didn't write anything," Matthew pleaded with Eddie. "You have to believe me."

"He didn't do it," Jenna said quietly. No one heard her.

"So you think I'm guilty too?" Eddie asked Matthew.

"No . . . yes . . . I just don't know."

"Of course you're guilty," Mike broke in. "Right guys?"

Mike had that look on his face -- either you're with me or against me.

"Sure," Kyle said quickly. "You got it right, Mike."

"Anything you say," JC mumbled.

Dan shook his head and refused to speak.

Sara gleefully hung on to Mike's arm.

"I thought . . ." Eddie choked. His eyes glistened with tears.

"I don't know," Matthew implored him to understand. "I have to think it through."

Eddie shook his head. He threw the sponge and rags on top of the ketchup and ran from the table. Mike laughed loudly.

"See, guys," Mike demanded. "Now you *know* he's guilty. An innocent guy doesn't run."

Dan and JC reluctantly shook their heads.

"I think you're right," Kyle said as he clicked off his tiny black tape recorder. He seemed to have enough story to satisfy him.

"Of course, I'm right," Mike bellowed, "I always am."

Chapter Ten
The Pact

Mike *wasn't* always right, but Matthew didn't have the nerve to say it out loud. Instead, he thought about it all the way home from the **Blitz**.

Four hours later Matthew was still thinking about it. He should have been working on his paper. Instead, he was sitting in his bedroom in front of the computer, seeing the words over and over again in his mind:

EDDIE'S SCAM

He saw them shimmering in blood red ketchup on the table at the **Blitz** and the contempt in Mike's eyes. Matthew stared at his hand and could see a red stain, even though there was nothing left of the ketchup. It was as if he were unable to let go of the image in his mind. Even worse, Matthew could actually *feel* Eddie's excruciating pain and his overwhelming compulsion to run.

At one time, Matthew had run away from his problems too. He quickly discovered that running didn't solve anything. The only solution is face up to what is happening and unravel the mystery. It was a tough lesson. Like Matthew, Eddie was going to learn it the hard way.

Matthew shrugged. He couldn't think about that now. It was Wednesday night and they had spent too much time at the **Blitz**. His paper was due Friday, and he wasn't finished. Matthew was having a lot of trouble putting the pieces together. He had plenty of information but he just couldn't make it work. There were missing links that he hadn't been able to locate on the internet or in his notes.

I really need Eddie's help, Matthew thought. After the **Blitz**, Matthew was convinced that Eddie would be shunning *him*. Why would Eddie help him with the paper now? Because of the ketchup on Matthew's hand, Eddie believed that Matthew had written on the table. It seemed that ketchup was always getting Matthew in trouble.

Maybe he should switch to mustard?

Matthew smiled as Gizmo made a failed attempt to leap into his lap. Gizmo was nearly thirty pounds now and far too big to sit in his lap. It didn't stop Gizmo from trying, Matthew thought, ruffling the puppy's curly fur. Gizmo sat back on the floor and stared at Matthew, tilting his head to one side.

"You trying to tell me something?" Matthew asked Gizmo.

Gizmo whimpered.

Matthew sat up straight. "You are trying to tell me something."

Gizmo heatedly wagged his tail.

"*What?*" Matthew insisted.

Gizmo whimpered again.

Matthew laughed out loud. "I'm asking a dog to talk to me? Am I nuts or something?"

He turned back to the papers on the desk next to the computer. There were piles of printouts about Hiram Bingham. There were stories about his famous family and his childhood in Hawaii. One printout discussed his tenure at Yale - teaching kids just like Mom and . . . Matthew paused. Teaching kids just like Mom and Eddie's dad. They were all teachers, like Mrs. Lash in Spanish and Mr. Richie in Social Studies. Matthew suddenly remembered what Mr. Richie had said about the scam warning posted on the school's online bulletin board.

It was posted on Monday, March 15th. Do you guys know what March 15th is? It's called the Ides of March. You might remember it from reading Shakespeare's Julius Caesar in English class. The soothsayer or fortuneteller says to Caesar, "Beware the Ides of March." That's because Caesar is going to be killed that day. Caesar ignored the warning. Ever since then, the Ides of March are foreboding -- just like the post that says beware.

Matthew searched his mind for the answer.

Was the post only a warning against the scam? Or was it more? Maybe it was part of the scam itself, designed to protect the cybercrook? Why use the Ides of March? *Caesar was going to be killed that day*. Was the post telling everyone that someone would be sacrificed in the scam? Was the victim Eddie?

Matthew stared at Gizmo.

If Eddie was the victim, how could he be the cybercrook too?

It didn't make sense. Nothing seemed to make sense. Who posted the warning on the Ides of March? Was he the same person as the cybercrook or simply a Good Samaritan?

There were too many scattered pieces, like his paper, that needed to be connected. Ironically, he required Eddie to accomplish both jobs.

Gizmo smiled.

"Dogs don't smile," Matthew said to the puppy.

Gizmo smiled anyway.

Matthew was going to say something when the doorbell rang.

Gizmo tensed and started barking. Downstairs, Mom opened the door. Matthew could hear voices but not identify who was speaking. Mom finally called up to him.

"Eddie is here to see you."

"Coming," Matthew said and pushed his chair away from the computer. It felt like a rerun. Why had Eddie come to *him* again?

Eddie stood in the foyer, shifting his weight back and forth. He was wearing a gray tee shirt and washed out jeans. Although it was cool out, Eddie was sweating.

"Yo," Matthew said.

Eddie looked up and nodded.

Mom smiled. "I'll go back to my work," she said, leaving them alone.

There was a long silence. Matthew was determined not to be the first one to speak.

Eddie rubbed his hands together. "I want to talk," he said finally.

"Yeah," Matthew mumbled.

"I mean, I really want to talk."

Matthew shook his head.

Eddie looked worn and haggard. "Why did you do it?"

"Do what?"

"Write *Eddie's Scam* in ketchup at the **Blitz**. Why did you do that to me? I thought we were friends?"

"I didn't do it," Matthew said with conviction. "You just don't want to believe me."

"You had ketchup on your hands. I saw it with my own eyes. What should I believe?"

Once again, Matthew recalled what it felt like to be so alone, with no one who believed you were innocent. Eddie probably felt like that now - if he was innocent. If he was guilty, then it was all a very clever decoy.

"Mike did it," Matthew said.

Eddie shrugged. "That's what I expected you to say."

"If you're my friend, you would know I could never do something like that."

"If you're my friend," Eddie echoed, "you know I could never be a cybercrook."

They glared at one another. Matthew was the first to look away.

Eddie held a paper in front of Matthew's eyes. "Did you see this?"

"What?"

"*The Rhodes Reporter*. Did you read it?"

"No."

"Here's what they're saying about me. Really bad stuff."

"What are you talking about?"

Eddie handed the paper to Matthew. Matthew read slowly, barely able to believe the topic that was reported.

The Rhodes Reporter

SPECIAL REPORT!

Why Would A Classmate Want to Scam You!

By Kyle Harris, Editor-in-Chief

This is a Special Report for The Rhodes Reporter. I interviewed students at Rhodes Middle School and asked for their opinions on why a classmate might want to scam them. Here's what they said:

I think a scammer would do it so she could buy a nice gift for her boyfriend. She probably didn't have enough money so she had to go to extremes.
Stuart Rubinstein

A girl would scam her friends because she would want more money so people wouldn't make fun of her. She might be wearing hand-me-downs, and she might also want to re-do her room. Maybe her sister or best friend worked with her and then they would split the money.
Kelly McCarthy

A guy would do it to prove he was cool and could hang out with popular kids.
Michael Greenbaum

A classmate might scam you to get revenge on some kids and their friends. He almost might want to get money to buy new things that would make him popular.
Christine Berghorn

A girl might be afraid that another girl would steal her boyfriend. She might set up a scam to get money to buy gifts for her boyfriend and bribe him to stay with her.
Katherine DiMaggio

FREE!
Bring this coupon to the Burger Blitz and get one free chocolate shake with an order of 6.5 hamburgers.

Good until 2043

Mustard or Ketchup?

By Breanna Wills

Most people use ketchup for everything! They put it on hamburgers and fries, eggs and pancakes, even on (ugh) spaghetti. It comes in really weird colors now, like green and purple.

No one ever thinks about mustard! Mustard goes really well with hot dogs, so why not with fries? We use it on a lot of sandwiches, and it doesn't get all red and drippy like ketchup. Even better, most people don't know that there's a lot of mustard in Chinese food. So the next time you're at the Blitz, go for the mustard not the ketchup.

"They're not talking about you." Matthew argued.

"Yeah, sure."

"Maybe you have a guilty conscience?"

There was a long silence.

Eddie cleared his throat. "How is the paper going?"

"Bad. I can't seem to get the pieces together. It's just not working."

"I know what you mean."

The silence hung in the air between them like a thick, impenetrable wall.

"You need help?" Eddie asked finally.

"Yeah."

Eddie looked everywhere but into Matthew's eyes. Matthew gazed at his sneakers, thinking about how he needed a new pair. The cross-trainers he wanted were simply too expensive - Mom refused to pay that much money for a pair of shoes. Before he shelled out the thirty dollars for the paper, Matthew was going to use his puppy-sitting money to help pay for them. He shuddered just *thinking* about the thirty dollars.

"Listen," Eddie said, his voice barely audible.

"What?"

"Listen," Eddie said louder. "Why don't we make a pact?"

"A pact?"

"Yeah."

"I don't know what you mean."

"What if I help you and you help me?"

"What are you talking about?"

"It seems that we're both in a mess right now. You need as much help from me as I need from you. What if I help you finish the paper and you help me figure this stuff out?"

"I'm not sure . . ."

"Listen, Matthew," Eddie's voice was urgent. "What do I have to gain by helping you? I'm in a big enough mess myself. I should be worrying about myself, not your problem. If we make a pact between friends, it will work for both of us."

"What do you want me to do?"

"Help me find the real cybercrook."

Matthew looked at him quizzically.

"OK, I know you're still not convinced I'm innocent. I can live with that because if you help me, we'll find who did it."

"Does that mean you're willing to believe I didn't do the ketchup at the **Blitz**?"

"Does that mean you're willing to believe I didn't sell the papers?"

They were at an impasse. Suddenly Gizmo barked and leaped up at Matthew. "What are you trying to tell me, dog?" Matthew grinned. Gizmo broke the tension.

Gizmo went over to Eddie and licked his hand.

Suddenly it was all very clear. "I don't have to believe you," Matthew said breathlessly, "and you don't have to believe me. We just need to agree that we're both innocent until proven guilty."

Eddie nodded. "It works for me."

"You'll help me finish my paper?"

"No problem."

"I'll help you figure out who is really guilty?"

"You got it."

Matthew stuck out his hand. "Deal."

Eddie gripped Matthew's hand. "I'll put thirty bucks down on this pact."

Matthew froze.

"Just kidding," Eddie said.

Matthew was not convinced.

Chapter Eleven
Morf

Hours later, after piles of printouts, searches on the internet and two drafts, they finished. Matthew had his paper; and Eddie had his pact.

"Now," Eddie said, "it's my turn."

Matthew had this odd sensation that he was like the lead in an old movie where the guy sells his soul to the devil to get the kind of life he really wants. At the end of the movie, the guy regrets selling his soul but it's too late. The pact had already been made.

Matthew wondered if he had sold his soul to get his paper in on time.

"That's our deal," Matthew agreed.

"Where do we start?"

Eddie's eyes reflected the light of the computer screen giving them a sinister Halloween-like glow.

"I'm not sure."

"We have to start someplace," Eddie persisted. "Right away. Look, I helped you. Don't you know anyone who can help us? You're supposed to be good at this kind of thing. Maybe there's someone on the outside, not involved with Mr. Richie's class or Rhodes Middle School - someone we can trust to work with us?"

Matthew tried to think of people that could help him. Maybe his friends from the *Tangled Web* could give them some ideas? He thought about all their stories and was simply too tired to hear them right now. He needed focus. That was the kind of direction Morf could give him.

"Morf!" Matthew said out loud. "Of course."

Eddie looked at him strangely. "What's a Morf?"

Matthew smiled affectionately. "Morf is the webmaster of *Tangled Web*, my favorite chat room. You know, like a host. No one ever meets Morf. Morf just likes to watch over us."

"What kind of a name is that?"

"Morf?" Matthew laughed again. "You know how he describes himself?"

"No?"

Matthew grinned as he repeated the words he memorized a long time ago.

"They call me Morf. Morf means I'm anything you need me to be. **M**ale **OR F**emale, lazy or lively, breakfast or dinner. There's a whole family of morfs in cyberspace. We change like the fish, swimming one minute, the next minute breaded on your bun from McDonald's . . . with fries on the side."

Eddie shrugged. "Weird."

"That's Morf."

"Why ask him?"

"Morf knows everything. He's always in cyberspace looking over your shoulder, knowing how to figure out the toughest mysteries."

Eddie shifted uncomfortably. "Is he really the best one to ask?"

"No question."

"I'm not sure."

"I am," Matthew said sternly.

"What if he knows too much?"

"What do you mean?"

"Well, what if he sees too much - you know, gets around like a hacker or cybersneak?"

"You could trust Morf. Don't worry about him."

"Isn't that illegal?" Eddie rubbed his hands together nervously.

"Morf doesn't do anything *illegal*. He helps direct you to solving problems on and off-line."

"Ok," Eddie acquiesced. "Let's e-mail Morf."

"I want to IM him right now," Matthew said. "Morf is usually online."

"Go ahead," Eddie sighed as Matthew typed the IM.

Hoops: Hi Morf.
Morf: Hi Hoops.
Hoops: I'm here with my friend, Eddie. He and I made a pact to help each other.
Morf: Friends?
Hoops: Yeah, Eddie is my friend. He just helped me write my paper. Now it's my turn to help him.
Morf: Sounds fair.
Hoops: First, I want to tell you the facts. You need to understand why Eddie had to help me.
Morf: I'm listening.

Matthew told Morf the whole story about the e-mail, the papers, the $30, and Gizmo's discovery. He described the warning posted on the school's online bulletin board, Mike blaming Eddie, and the kids getting very angry.

Morf: Eddie has big problems.
Hoops: I know. I promised I would help him. Eddie knows that I believe people are innocent until proven guilty. I need to find some proof - either way. What do you think I should do?
Morf: Let me think about this. After all, the cybercrook committed a very big crime and the kids committed a smaller crime, even though they were lucky not to get caught.
Hoops: I know.
Morf: Whoever sold the papers has a lot of money.

*Illustration Credit:*Loretta Jacobs

Hoops: Yes.
Morf: They also have a list of all the people who bought the paper - even though they haven't used it again -- yet.

Matthew shivered.

Hoops: Yes.
Morf: If the cybercrook gets away with it and keeps all the money he still has your name and e-mail on his blackmail list.
Hoops: That's a scary thought.
Morf: There's only one thing you can do.
Hoops: What?
Morf: There are tangled trails that may or may not lead you to the cybercrook. They're like paths in a maze - some are dead ends, others give you clues and the one real trail will take you directly to the cybercrook.
Hoops: Where do I begin?
Morf: The first trail to follow is sniffing out the money. You know how the FBI followed the money trail of the terrorists so they could figure out who paid for their plot?
Hoops: Yes.
Morf: Do the same thing. Look around - is anyone spending a lot of money? Is anyone buying new electronics, expensive clothing or accessories, or a lot of unnecessary stuff?
Hoops: That doesn't sound too hard.
Morf: Following the money is a lot harder than you think.
Hoops: I'll do it.
Morf: The second trail to follow is tracking the paper. If Eddie wrote it and didn't sell it, then someone must have stolen it. Follow the paper through all the rough drafts to see who, what, where, when, why, and how it was stolen. Beware of scam artists that pop up everywhere - not just on the Ides of March. Once they have you tangled in their grip, you're part of the their web. They have your name, your e-mail, and your intended crime. That's enough to keep them coming back for more. The situation might get much worse before it gets better.
Hoops: Any other options?
Morf: Not one you'll want to hear. Sometimes being objective

isn't easy for friends.
Hoops: I'm asking you for ALL the possibilities with no strings attached. I want to find the truth.
Morf: You have to consider the possibility that the paper wasn't stolen. Perhaps the person who *wrote* the paper also sold it. Maybe you've become part of it. If you pursue the cybercrook with Eddie then it looks like you're both innocent. Both of you may not be innocent. You could be part of a very clever cover-up.

There was nothing left to say. Matthew walked Eddie to the front door.

"We're going to find this guy, right?" Eddie said hopefully.

"Sure," Matthew mumbled. "I'll see you in school tomorrow."

Eddie nodded. He walked slowly down the front path and onto the sidewalk. He stopped suddenly, staring across the street. Matthew followed Eddie's gaze.

"Yo, Nicole," Eddie waved. Nicole was just coming home. She waved at Eddie and crossed the street to say hello.

Nicole and Matthew watched Eddie walk down the street. Suddenly, Nicole pointed to a cluster of bushes. "Who's that?"

Matthew squinted into the darkness. There was definitely someone watching them.

"I don't know."

Unexpectedly, the person crept out of the shadows and followed Eddie.

"It looks like Dylan - but I'm not sure." Matthew said. "He's probably taking a shortcut from the library."

"Who's Dylan?"

"Nobody," Matthew replied. "He's just the class loner. No one pays much attention to him."

"From what I've heard, people are paying too much attention to Eddie."

Matthew nodded sadly. "I just can't figure it out." Matthew told her about the pact, how Eddie helped him write the paper, and their IM with Morf.

"It's not finished," Nicole frowned.

"What do you mean?"

"I've been hearing all these stories about Eddie getting pushed around school. Mike is bullying him, right?"

Matthew nodded.

"I think Morf had more to say. He just couldn't do it while Eddie was looking over your shoulder."

"What should I do?"

"Let's go online and see if we can find Morf again."

Matthew agreed.

Hoops: Hi Morf.
Morf: Hi.
Hoops: I got the feeling you had more to say. Eddie isn't here anymore. Nicole is.
Morf: Good.
Hoops: Is there something else you wanted to tell me?
Morf: Yeah, there is.
Hoops: What is it?
Morf: You have to be careful. And Eddie has to be even more careful.
Hoops: I don't understand.
Morf: No one knows for sure that Eddie is guilty, right?
Hoops: Right.
Morf: Yet Mike and his friends are already bullying him.
Hoops: Yeah.
Morf: It doesn't matter whether he's guilty or not.
Hoops: No?
Morf: That's because in a way, you're all guilty. If you and the others didn't buy the paper then they wouldn't have lost the money.
Hoops: We were victims.
Morf: Victims AND perpetrators.
Hoops: I don't understand.
Morf: You were victims of the internet hoax, right?
Hoops: Yeah.
Morf: Would you have been victims if you turned the paper in?
Hoops: What do you mean?
Morf: You were willing to commit a crime, too. The crime was plagiarism. So the victims were also the potential perpetrators.

Hoops: [sigh] I see what you mean.
Morf: Kids who bought the paper should take responsibility for that, at least.
Hoops: So?
Morf: They're not. Instead, they're picking on Eddie.
Hoops: They believe he sold them the papers.
Morf: You're missing the point. They don't want to believe that they share in the guilt. It's easier to pin it on someone else. Then they don't have to think about it. In their own mind, they come across as innocent victims.
Hoops: Oh. You mean it's like the kid from RCC who got expelled. He probably thought he was just using the internet as a resource when it was really plagiarism.
Morf: You got it.
Hoops: I'm not sure I like it.
Morf: You shouldn't. You're one of them.
Hoops: I'm not picking on Eddie.
Morf: You're not defending him, either.
Hoops: Mike is the bully - not me!!!!!!!
Morf: Mike can't be a bully without the rest of you.
Hoops: I don't understand.
Morf: You will. Just watch what happens. If all the kids had zero tolerance for bullies there would be no Mikes in school.
Hoops: I don't get it.
Morf: Watch what happens. You'll get it fast enough. Gotta go now.
Hoops: [shrugs] I still don't get it.
Morf: Keep your eyes and mind open. One more thought. This whole scam can be a scheme to frame Eddie.
Hoops: Why?
Morf: Eddie may have some serious enemies.
Hoops: Impossible. He's only been at Rhodes for 6 weeks. And he's a great basketball player, too.
Morf: You never know. People don't always recognize their enemies.

The Rhodes Reverie

Friday, March 19

Welcome to the Rhodes Middle School online bulletin board. Post your ideas, thoughts, and adventures! Leave messages for friends and talk about your favorite classes!

>party@Lindsay's. Casual Dress. 7:00 sharp.

>Revenge on RCC and all their teachers!

>Bully Advice: you wouldn't like it if it was happening to you. "STOP BULLYING"

>I don't think there should be such a thing as "the popular group" and other groups too.

>I think the cafeteria should get better lunches, I found a hair in my bagel.

Chapter Twelve
What's New?

The papers were due and terrible things began to happen.

Morf's words ran through Matthew's mind over and over again, like an annoying jingle he couldn't stop.

Just watch what happens. If all the kids had zero tolerance for bullies, there would be no Mikes in school.

Between first and second period Mike "accidentally" crashed into Eddie, sending his books flying in all directions. Some kids laughed, others stepped on Eddie's papers.

Between fourth and fifth period, Mike, Kyle, JC and Robby cornered Eddie outside the gym. Matthew watched as Mike jabbed him with his finger, tossed his backpack across the hall, and taunted him with names like *Latino* boy. Eddie cowered as they surrounded him, his eyes filled with fear.

Kyle held his tiny black tape recorder and laughed with Robby and JC. Matthew did nothing. Dylan paused, gawking. The other kids in the hallway paused, creating a crunch with everyone trying to squeeze around and get a better look.

Matthew couldn't believe that JC was following Mike, cheering him as he pushed Eddie. JC was a gentle guy - he was never mean or acted like a bully. Everyone *liked* JC. Yet there he was with the others, laughing, teasing, and pushing Eddie around. Matthew wondered if it was all part of Mike's plans. He remembered what Mike had said at the **Blitz**:

"Stay away from him," Mike had ordered the group, "until we can figure out a way to get our money back."

Suddenly Eddie's eyes found Matthew.

Help me.

Matthew's jaw fell open as Eddie pleaded with his eyes.

Help me.

Mike turned and followed Eddie's gaze. He glared at Matthew. "Going to join us Hooper?" Mike asked cuttingly.

Matthew looked at Mike, JC, and Kyle. They paused, waiting for Matthew to move.

Help me, Eddie implored silently.

Mike's eyes were ice. "You're either with us," he snarled, "or with him. What's your choice, Hooper?"

Matthew's heart pounded. Mike was wrong. The real question was whether Eddie was the cybercrook.

"Make your choice," Mike stepped away from Eddie. He walked straight up to Matthew until their faces were inches apart. "Are you with your buddies?" Mike's voice was a deep rumble like thunder right before a lightening storm. "Or maybe you have my money, too. Maybe, Hooper, you're partners with this slime . . ."

Matthew opened his mouth to speak. He wanted to tell Mike that he had nothing to do with the papers, that he wasn't sure about Eddie, but bullying him was no way to get to the truth. He wanted to tell Mike about Morf, and how he had put Matthew on the trail, determined to sniff out the real cybercrook.

No words came.

Matthew stared helplessly at Mike. Matthew wasn't a fighter, and everyone knew how effective Mike was with his fists. There was no doubt that Matthew would lose.

Mike was a mass of tensed muscle waiting to pounce. From the sidelines, Dylan was still standing and gawking. Matthew found himself taking the same stance.

In the corner of his eye, Matthew saw JC, Kyle and Robby watching eagerly. Eddie was still begging with his eyes, *help me*.

Matthew could hardly breathe.

Unexpectedly, Mr. Harvey emerged from the gym. He was the physical education teacher.

"What's going on here?" Mr. Harvey demanded.

Mike backed away. "Nothing."

"Nothing?" Mr. Harvey persisted.

"Nothing," Mike mumbled.

"Then get to class. Now."

The boys scattered.

Matthew forced his feet to move, barely able to focus on where he was going. Someone grabbed his arm. Matthew glanced at the kid next to him. It was Kyle.

"We'll be late for class," Kyle steered Matthew toward the steps.

Matthew shook his head. He had to ask the question. "Why did you do it?"

"Do what?"

"Let Mike pick on Eddie."

"Let Mike do what?" Kyle looked confused.

"Let Mike pick on Eddie," Matthew repeated. "You backed Mike all the way."

"So? I always back a winner."

"What does that have to do with Eddie?" Matthew countered.

"I was just watching," Kyle frowned. "I didn't do anything."

Matthew looked at him incredulously. "Are you kidding?"

Kyle shook his head. "I don't know what you're talking about. JC, Robby and I were just watching to see what Eddie would say. After all, we lost thirty bucks too." Kyle caught himself. "Hey, even Dylan stuck around trying to get his money back."

Matthew paused in the doorway to class. Could it possibly be true? Could JC, Robby, and Kyle not realize that they were helping Mike bully Eddie?

It was startling to even think of that possibility.

Out of the blue, Matthew recalled Mr. Richie's words.

It's natural for people to want to be part of a group . . . Groups are a very good thing unless they become cruel, maliciously leave people out, or work together to hurt another person or group. Sometimes people in a group lose their individuality and go along with the crowd, not realizing the ramifications of what they're doing.

Kyle had been part of the group following Mike. He didn't even realize that like Mike, he had become a bully. Matthew shivered. The situation was getting too complicated. He had to find the real cybercrook quickly, and make sure the kids got their money back before Mike lost control and the "group" became really dangerous. There were so many stories about gangs attacking people, hurting them, even . . . Matthew took a deep breath . . . killing them. He couldn't imagine Mike, Kyle, JC, and Robby killing anyone. Then again you never know for sure. Matthew had read a true story about a boy named Phillip who was constantly threatened, pushed around, and humiliated by kids at school. Terrified of the bullies, afraid to tell his parents or the school, Phillip didn't know what to do. Unable to bear it, he went home one day and killed himself.

Matthew shuddered. Eddie wasn't tough or mean. Even if Eddie was guilty, it could have the same result. Bullying was dangerous for both the victim and the bullies. Suddenly Matthew felt as if they were all stumbling into a dark, treacherous hole, and if someone didn't find a way out soon, there would be no turning back.

Matthew didn't hear a thing in class. Next period was lunch and he planned to see if he could slow down the kids. Matthew wanted to convince them not to do anything until he could figure out whom the cybercrook was, and how they could get back their money.

Everything went wrong from the beginning.

It was macaroni-and-cheese day in the cafeteria, and everyone hated the yellow, gooey mess they called pasta. Matthew sat at a long table with Mike, Jenna, JC, Kyle, Dan, Alyssa, Sara, and Breanna. He wanted to calmly reason with them. They were all too angry.

"Did you get Mr. Richie's paper done?" Kyle asked the group.

"No," Mike snarled. "I have to turn it in late. Kyle can't write it until the weekend."

"That means you take one grade lower to begin with," Sara said acidly. "If Kyle really wanted to help you, he would have gotten it in on time."

"Yeah," Mike grumbled, "all because of Eddie."

"Nobody's going to get a good grade on *that* paper," Robby sighed.

"We're all taking the final," Breanna sneered at Sara.

"Lousy break," JC sighed.

"Except for you," Sara glanced at Jenna.

"I never bought the paper to begin with," Jenna defended herself. "I didn't have the money."

Matthew was silent.

"What about *you*?" Sara persisted. She stared at Matthew.

"Yeah, Hooper, what about your paper?" Mike glared.

"I . . ."

"He wrote his own paper," Jenna interceded.

Matthew looked at her quizzically. How did she know that?

"Are you so smart," Mike demanded, "that you can write a whole paper in such a short time? Maybe you're rich enough to buy *another* paper?"

Matthew began to say something when Robby jumped in.

"I heard," Robby said, "that Eddie helped Matthew finish his paper."

All eyes turned to Matthew.

"Is that true?" Mike demanded.

Matthew was at a loss for words.

"Is that true?" Mike asked again.

Matthew opened his mouth. Yeah, he wanted to say. *Yeah it's true Eddie helped me because he thinks we're friends. We have a pact - he helped me write my paper, and I'm going to help him find the real cybercrook.*

"Is that true?" Kyle asked.

"Is that true?" JC asked.

Help me, Eddie had pleaded with his eyes.

"Is that true?" Jenna echoed the others.

"No," Matthew said in someone else's voice. "No, Eddie didn't help me write the paper. I wrote it myself."

Matthew lied. Again. The conversation shifted immediately.

"Eddie really messed us up," Mike scowled. "I have my people out there tracing his e-mail. You know, the one he sent us offering the paper? They're going to follow it right back to that *Latino boy's* computer, and then we'll know how to get our thirty bucks back."

Everyone nodded enthusiastically.

"We're not going to let him get away with this," Mike snarled.

"We're not going to let him get away with this," Kyle echoed Mike.

"No way," the others said simultaneously.

"C'mon," Mike stood up from the table, "let's take this outside."

They all stood and followed Mike.

Jenna touched Matthew's arm lightly. "Stay with me," she whispered.

Jenna and Matthew hung back, pretending to slowly empty their trays.

"What do you want?" Matthew asked, lowering his voice.

"Look," Jenna glanced across the lunchroom.

Matthew followed her gaze. Eddie was slowly approaching them. Matthew held his breath, praying that Mike wouldn't turn around and see them talking to Eddie.

Eddie stopped in front of them. "What about the pact?" He asked Matthew.

"What pact?" Jenna's voice was soft.

"We have a pact," Eddie turned to Jenna. "Matthew and I made a deal that I would help him with his paper and he would help me find the cybercrook."

Jenna stared at Matthew. "*Eddie* helped you with the paper?"

Matthew nodded miserably, unable to meet her eyes.

"He spoke to Morf," Eddie continued. "Morf is his online buddy - you know someone who knows *everything* that goes on in cyberspace?"

Jenna nodded, her eyes still fixed on Matthew.

"Morf told us to follow the trail."

"Follow the trail?"

"Sniff out clues," Eddie explained.

Eddie didn't mention *his* name, Matthew thought.

"Good idea," Jenna said enthusiastically. "Let's start with the money. We can check out who has been buying new stuff."

The strangest things began to happen.

"You have new sneakers, Eddie." Jenna observed. "They're just like Mike's."

"I bought them with money I earned at the **Blitz**," Eddie said defensively. "Did you notice that Mike has a brand new MP3 player? Do you know how much that costs?"

Jenna shrugged.

"Mike always has extra money," Matthew volunteered. "We all know that."

"Yeah," Jenna added, "but Kyle is wearing a new shirt. Did you guys see the label? You have any idea how much it costs?"

"Never noticed," Matthew mumbled.

"What about you?" Jenna demanded. "That's a leather backpack. They're expensive."

"I've had this all year," Matthew said defiantly.

"Robby has a new backpack too," Eddie added, "and a digital camera to match."

"He's a sports photographer," Matthew argued.

"How come he didn't use the school camera?"

"I heard that Sara got a new stereo," Jenna said.

"It was her birthday," Matthew interjected.

"Yeah," Eddie was excited. "Alyssa has been wearing a lot of those gold chains recently . . ."

"Breanna has a new silver locket . . ."

"A new locket?" Jenna asked.

"Yeah," Matthew squinted. "It looks just like the one that Mike gave to Sara, except it's silver."

"For someone who has no money, how did Breanna pay for it?" Eddie asked.

The three were silent.

"Look, JC has a new baseball glove. Doesn't that cost a lot of money?" Jenna asked.

"Stop!" Matthew shouted. "We're acting like a bunch of bullies. We should be following the money not picking on each other."

Jenna shrugged. "Hey, even Dylan over there has a new pen. Does that count?"

Eddie smiled.

Matthew heard Morf's words in his head.

Mike can't be a bully without the rest of you.

For the rest of the day, Matthew couldn't help looking at people. What about the crazy bus driver? Wasn't he wearing new combat boots tucked beneath his old camouflage fatigues? Even Mr. Richie was wearing a new watch. Matthew hated to lump them together, but did that make them both suspects?

My Plan
by Matthew

I Suspects
- Jenna - Dylan - Eddie? - Nicole
- JC - MIKE - Sarah

II My Plan
- wheresgeorge.com
- who has more things

III Help
- Nicole
- Mr. Richie
- Tangled Web

IV Problems
- S.S. paper due
- be a bystander or help Eddie
- Watch Gizmo
- Find cyberc[illegible]

Illustration Credit: Sofia-Marie Guttilla

Chapter Thirteen
Is The President A Bully?

School was over for the day. Most of the kids had gone home, met with clubs, or were playing intramurals on the fields. The hallway was empty, echoing like a heavy, hollow pipe tossed aside after a construction project. Matthew shivered. He should be home walking Gizmo and shooting hoops with Nicole. Instead he was drawn back to Mr. Richie's classroom, his mind bursting with questions. Mr. Richie seemed to know a lot about how people behaved. Maybe he could explain what Morf was trying to say? Morf's words nagged at Matthew - he instinctively knew that they were critical to solving the mystery of the cybercrook. But how? As hard as he tried, Matthew couldn't unravel the pieces.

Suddenly he found himself in front of Mr. Richie's classroom. Matthew peeked inside. Mr. Richie was alone, sitting at his desk and reading intently from a stack of papers. He had a red pen in his hand and was scrawling words across the sheets. Matthew wondered if he was grading the social studies papers. He recalled what Mr. Richie had said only last week about the mysterious online post:

I don't know what this post is saying. Obviously, the person who wrote it is trying to tell us something. Thirty dollars is a lot of money. I would imagine it's enough money to buy things you guys would want like a few CDs, a new computer game or even a paper off the internet. I think you should consider this message very carefully while I intend to obliterate it from my mind. However, if you need me, my door is always open . . ."

Mr. Richie's door was always open. He seemed to understand what was going on without making judgments or getting anyone in trouble. Maybe Mr. Richie could answer Matthew's questions.

Matthew took a deep breath. "Mr. Richie," he said weakly.

Mr. Richie looked up from his papers. "Matthew," he smiled. "What can I do for you?"

"Can I . . . talk to you? Just for a minute?"

Mr. Richie put down his pen. "Sure, c'mon in."

Matthew glanced around the classroom. It was empty. There was a strange, otherworldly feel about the empty classroom as if the kids had all sold their souls to . . . whom? Mike? The devil? Matthew shook his head. His imagination was getting away from him, scurrying into dark corners he didn't want to visit.

"Matthew?" Mr. Richie urged him.

Matthew took one hesitant step inside the classroom.

"Matthew," Mr. Richie laughed. "You're certainly not afraid of me?"

"Oh . . . no . . . that's not it at all," Matthew mumbled.

"So come in. Obviously, you want to ask me something."

Matthew took a deep breath and exhaled. He had to be very careful not to reveal the truth, just in case Mr. Richie would want to take further action . . .

"Talk to me."

"Well, you seem to know an awful lot about how kids . . . people . . . behave in groups."

"That's part of social studies."

"Oh."

"What do you want to know about . . . groups?"

"Well, hypothetically speaking, I mean. What if you have a group - maybe kids - picking on someone else? You know, maybe the group is right, and maybe the group is wrong. But they're picking on someone else and *that's* bad. Know what I mean?"

"I'm not exactly sure. It depends on what they're doing, how often, and who they're picking on."

"Oh."

"Are you talking about someone getting bullied, Matthew?"

"Yeah. I guess so."

"Is it you?"

"No."

"Is it someone you know?"

Matthew shook his head vigorously.

"Do you want to say his name?"

"No."

Mr. Richie narrowed his eyes and stared thoughtfully at Matthew. "Do you know anything about bullying?"

"No. Yes. I mean, I've been bullied at times. Hasn't everyone?"

"You're right, most people have. It's sad, too, because it doesn't really have to happen."

"I don't understand."

"You know how I talked about group behavior in class? How it's more like a force than an individual action? That's what bullying is about."

"Huh?"

"Bullying is more than one kid picking on another. It's about power, Matthew. One person wants to hold a lot of power in a group but he can't do it without help. In order to get the power he has to have everyone around supporting him. A bully needs the silent support of other kids, the vulnerability and fear of his victim, and the unspoken support of the adults."

"I don't get it."

"Look at it another way," Mr. Richie suggested. "It's like being President of the United States. That's the most powerful position in the world, right? But you don't just *become* president. First, you have to really want to get elected. You have to want the power. Then you need to show others in your political party that you're very strong. Finally, you secure the agreement or support of the majority of people in the country to elect you."

"What does that have to do with bullying?"

"The process of getting hold of power is essentially the same. The President does it through an acceptable legal process; the bully does it through brute force, but it basically follows the same trail."

"I don't understand, Mr. Richie."

"Let's look at it more carefully. How do Presidents get elected? They have their group or political party backing them. Then they have to campaign to get the millions of bystanders or voters in the country to support them. They devise a platform, plan, or cause to convince the majority to vote for them. Within that "cause" is a victim or enemy. A President might pick on a bad economy, a political enemy or terrorists. Whatever he chooses, it makes him look stronger, and the people supporting the president feel *empowered*. For example, most voters would support a war against terrorists, right?"

"Yeah, but that's a good thing."

"I know - that's why it makes the President *look* good."

"OK -- so the President of the United States is a bully?"

Mr. Richie laughed. "It's the same behavior in kids. Look at it this way. You get a kid who wants to have a lot of power over other kids. They're usually popular, strong, and impulsive. They like to defy the rules and view anyone who disagrees with them as hostile. Most kids are in awe or afraid of that."

Matthew thought of Mike.

"Bullies are very careful who they choose as victims. They're not going to attack strong, popular kids because it just won't work. If they do that, the bully can lose his power. Instead they go after loners, people who are different or vulnerable, new kids, and people who don't like to fight. They particularly like kids who respond so emotionally that they come back for more, always looking for a way out of the conflict."

Matthew thought of Eddie - new to the school, Hispanic, and reluctant to fight because of his family history.

"Just as important," Mr. Richie added, "are the bystanders. They're the silent majority. Those are all the kids who watch and do nothing. Sometimes they encourage a bully or just laugh and show approval. Keep in mind that the greatest fear of bystanders is that the bully will turn on them. If bystanders get picked on, they try to appease the bully, doing what he asks to avoid confrontation. Like all the voters that place a President in office, it's the bystanders who put and *keep* a bully in power."

Matthew thought of himself. He shuddered.

"Bullying hurts everyone," Mr. Richie continued. "If bullies are allowed to continue their behavior when they grow up, they are more likely to become criminals, get arrested, and be involved in family violence."

"For real?"

"Yeah, for real. People who are the target of bullies often become stressed out, fearful and physically sick. They become afraid of places like the school bathroom, the athletic fields, and the school bus because they might be bullied there. Victims often find it much harder to do schoolwork. Sometimes they turn dangerous when they try to seek revenge. That's what happened at Columbine High School when two victims of school bullies shot and killed 14 students, a teacher, and themselves."

Matthew shuddered.

"Then there are the bystanders," Mr. Richie said softly. "They often feel angry and helpless. They don't know what to do, but they feel guilty for doing nothing. Sometimes *they* have nightmares and are haunted by the idea that they'll be the next victims."

"I know what you mean," Matthew whispered.

Mr. Richie gazed at him silently.

Matthew took a deep breath. "So what can Ed . . ." he stopped.

Mr. Richie stared at him, waiting. "So what can Eddie do?"

Matthew was silent.

"Eddie is your friend, right? He's the one we're really talking about here?"

"I can't . . ."

"You don't have to say anything, Matthew. I figured as much."

Matthew shook his head miserably.

"He can tell an adult," Mr. Richie began. "He can look Mike in the eye and tell him to stop. And he can get away from the situation as quickly as possible and tell an adult what happened."

"Everyone would think he was a wimp," Matthew argued.

"That's a big part of the problem. You know how I said that the bully needs the unspoken support of the adults?"

Matthew nodded.

"Eddie needs to talk to the teachers and tell them he's being bullied, so when he asks for help they'll support him."

"I can't do it for him?"

"No. But you can tell him what to do."

"If I do, Mike will bully me."

"Maybe. But if you get your basketball buddies to stand by you, Mike will lose all his innocent bystanders. Then he's like a President without any votes."

Matthew was silent, trying to sort out his thoughts. "What happens," he said slowly, "if I'm not sure whether Eddie is guilty or innocent?"

Mr. Richie did not respond.

"I mean, Eddie is my friend but he *did* write the paper."

Mr. Richie nodded.

"So how do I know he didn't sell it?"

Mr. Richie waited.

"Did you read the first draft of Eddie's paper? The same one he turned in today?"

"Yes."

Matthew's heart pounded. "When?"

"He came by over two weeks ago, and we reviewed it on disk. We used the classroom computer. Eddie asked me to check it over because he really wanted a good grade."

Suddenly Matthew felt like a detective on television crime show. "What did you do with it?"

"I printed out a copy, then put it on my desk."

"Until when?"

"I took my lunch break but left it on the desk."

"Did you lock the room?"

Mr. Richie nodded.

"So it was on your desk *all* day, available to anyone except during lunch time."

"Yes."

"That means someone could have picked it up, copied it, and returned it later without you even knowing?"

"It's possible."

"*Anyone* could have stolen it?"

"It looks that way."

Matthew's mind was racing. "That means," he continued, thinking out loud, "that if the stolen paper was the same as the first draft, and Eddie's final copy is different . . ."

Mr. Richie nodded.

"Then the chances are likely Eddie *didn't* sell the papers on the internet."

"If I was really smart," a voice behind Matthew said bitterly, "I would have done just that."

Matthew swung around.

Eddie was standing at the classroom door.

"You heard everything?" Matthew asked.

"Yeah, I heard everything."

"I had to know," Matthew said weakly.

Eddie shrugged.

"Can I help you?" Mr. Richie asked Eddie.

"Yeah," Eddie mumbled. "I'm not feeling very good these days. So I thought I would get the homework for next week . . . just in case I'm sick and I can't make it into school."

Mr. Richie glanced knowingly at Matthew. "Are you sick?" Mr. Richie prodded gently.

"No . . . kind of, know what I mean? I'm getting these headaches and I feel . . ." Eddie let the words dangle in the air.

"Can I ask you a question Eddie?" Mr. Richie requested soothingly.

Eddie nodded.

"It's about your paper."

Eddie stared at the floor.

"Where do you keep the disk?"

"In my backpack," Eddie said firmly, "in the zipper compartment."

Mr. Richie nodded. "Where is it now?"

"Still in my backpack."

"Can I see it?"

"Sure." Eddie slipped off his backpack, unzipped it, and dug inside.

Eddie searched but the disk just wasn't there. That's when Eddie remembered that he tried to use it as proof for Mike. Eddie didn't know where it was.

Mr. Richie tried to help Eddie recall where the disk could be.

Matthew felt like he was on the other side of the one-way mirror in a police interrogation room. He could see everything that was happening but wasn't part of the action. Although he felt caught in the middle, Matthew slipped out of the room without anyone noticing him.

Chapter Fourteen
Tangled Talk

Matthew left Mr. Richie, Eddie, and the school. He was still very confused. All the things that Mr. Richie said about bullies made sense. Matthew wanted to know whether it was okay to bully someone who was a cybercrook. Was Eddie the cybercrook? The question plagued him. Obviously someone could have stolen the paper from Mr. Richie's desk or the disk from Eddie's backpack. Was Eddie smart enough to create two decoys or was the cybercrook laughing at all of them?

When Matthew approached his house he saw Nicole shooting hoops in her driveway. Matthew paused as she threw a perfect air ball.

"Yo, Matthew," Nicole said as she tossed the basketball. She never even looked at him.

"I need to talk to you," Matthew said sheepishly.

"Again?" Nicole teased.

"I'm serious."

"Don't you have to walk the dog?"

"Yeah. But this is more important."

Nicole caught the rebound and sprinted over to Matthew. "What's more important than taking care of that cute little puppy?"

"He's not *cute*," Matthew wrinkled his nose, "and he's not little either."

Nicole laughed.

"Anyway," Matthew grumbled, "I want you to listen to me. I know I can really trust you and I need to do . . . something. I just don't know what *something* is."

Nicole patted him on the arm. "Sure, I'm listening."

Matthew gazed into Nicole's eyes. He could always count on her. "OK," he began. Matthew gave her an update. "I still don't know where to go."

"It's a tough one," Nicole nodded solemnly. "Here's what I would do. Go home and take care of Gizmo. When you're finished, I'll meet you at your house, and we'll hit the computer."

"To do what?"

"Ask the experts. Who knows more about bullies, e-bullies, and blank

disks than the kids on Tangled Web?"
"You're right," Matthew grinned. "Let's do it."

Matthew and Nicole sat in front of the computer. Gizmo sat at their feet. Matthew logged online.

Welcome to the Tangled Web
Hoops enters the room.

Gigs> Yo Hoops.
Media> How u doing?
Wheels> Hows your problems?
Red> N E good stories? :-)

Matthew glanced at Nicole.

Hoops>i learned a lot about bullying today.
Media>i hate bullies. A kid in my grade was beat up because the bullies thought he was a loser. The bullies were suspended but the kid still suffered.
Red>Bad stuff.
Wheels>u think that's bad? There's an LD kid in my school and sometimes we c him in the hallways. He loves football and his favorite team is the Green Bay Packers. If u say the name of Green Bay's biggest enemies, the Chicago Bears, this kid goes crazy. Today i saw some kids around him chanting "Bears rule" over and over again, just 2 torture him. They laughed when he got mad.
Red>That stuff happens around my school 2. My friend was walking home from school 1 day with her very *expensive* Kate Spade pocketbook. A kid from school threatened her with a fake gun 2 give it up and she did. She reported it 2 the principal and the police arrested the guy. It turned out that the creep was doing it to lots of girls, and everyone was afraid 2 say anything. My friend never wears expensive things anymore because she is so damaged.
Hoops>Not all kids r bad.

Gigs>Get real. Most kids aren't bad.
Media>Most kids aren't bullies, either.
Hoops>Most kids avoid them.
Gigs>Yeah? i know this kid, Jon, who was 1 of the most popular guys in school. He had a lot of friends, including Colin. Colin was a real nerd - one hundred averages, glasses, braces, all that stuff. Everyone teased Jon about being friends with Colin. So Jon stopped asking Colin 2 hang out with him. Colin was really, really upset because it happened regularly. One night Colin called Jon and told him that he was going 2 bring a bomb 2 school and kill himself. Colin said he hated his life. Jon told him not 2 do it. They talked 4 about 3 hours and Jon and Colin have been best friends since.
Red>Jon sounds really cool.
Gigs>The real bullies were the kids picking on Colin. They tease NE 1 who looks different, wears different clothes, or has a different lifestyle. In my school they picked on another kid just because he came from a different country!
Media>Once i had a friend who would just joke around with me because I'm Hispanic. She made fun of me all the time. She was only joking but it made me really mad because the jokes were not funny. She was really hurtful. She wouldn't stop when i asked and i knew she would just make fun of me more if I told on her -- so I kept it 2 myself.
Hoops>u should have told someone.
Media>Who?
Hoops>A teacher?
Media> lol
Hoops> Anyone ever hear of an e-bully?
Wheels>u should know all about that.
Gigs>i know this kid who can hack onto peoples screen names and can shut them offline! He can also shut down someone's computer by giving it a virus. There are a lot of people who have been mistreated online and don't know who they're talking 2. Is that what u mean by an e-bully?

Matthew and Nicole looked at one another.

Hoops>Yeah.
Red>i have the best e-bully story of all!
Gigs>i didn't know we were competing.
Red>shut it down. A girl in my class opened a forum with different topics. They were all appropriate like the nicest teacher and best restaurant. Then things got nasty. Biggest stuck-up, ugliest person, etc. started 2 show up. People got very upset and offended. They blamed the girl who opened the site. Of course it wasn't her fault but she still got blamed. Everybody was really angry! The e-bullies ruined her website!

"I think I've heard enough stories," Nicole sighed.

Matthew nodded. Although Mr. Richie hadn't been online, the kids from Tangled Web proved his point.

"I think it's time to let everything that happened this week sink in," Nicole advised. "Tomorrow is Saturday, and you can spend the whole weekend thinking. It will give you time to answer some of your questions about this whole mess."

"I think you're right," Matthew mumbled. "We need some time to let this all blow over. Then everything will go back to normal."

The Rhodes Reverie

Sunday, March 21

Welcome to the Rhodes Middle School online bulletin board. Post your ideas, thoughts, and adventures! Leave messages for friends and talk about your favorite classes!

>Lost dog: brought in for show and tell. $2,000 reward. Last seen on the streets of Philadelphia.

>You're headed for trouble. Watch those pesos!

>There is a really big bully problem in our school. I wish it could stop.

>Rock band looking for new bassist and drummer. Experience needed.

>Drama club tryouts tomorrow, bring script

Chapter Fifteen
In The Dark

Matthew turned the light off in his bedroom, burrowing deep beneath the covers. Gizmo leaped up on the bed, curling comfortably at Matthew's feet. It was Sunday night. He had taken Nicole's advice and spent the weekend thinking about everything that had happened during the week. The last thing he did on his computer was to check his inbox. Matthew was stunned when he read the e-mail:

```
To: Matthew
From: A friend
Subject: Your money
Date: Sunday, March 21

Hi Matthew.

i know who sold u the paper on Machu Picchu. i
also know how 2 get your money back. i need $5
2 pay the hacker who will break into the
cybercrook's computer 2 get u the proof as
well as find out exactly where the money is.
If u r buying, leave $5 under your front
doormat and i will e-mail u the proof, and how
2 get the money by 4PM Monday.

I'm sure u will know exactly what 2 do with
all this info. However, I'm only making this
offer to *YOU* u must keep this a secret
between the 2 of us. If u tell NE 1 else the
deal is off!!!!

Dont worry - i will know if u let our secret
out.
```

Suddenly, Nicole's advice came to fruition. All of Matthew's questions about the cybercrook would finally be answered.

He believed the e-mail would reveal all the information he needed. Matthew would find out everything tomorrow. He would solve the mystery, stop the bullying, and get back all the money. If the e-mail was another scam, he had that covered too. He recalled what Nicole had asked when she found out Matthew had bought the paper off the internet.

You did mark the money?

Matthew smiled in the darkness. He remembered the conversation on the Tangled Web when he told them he didn't mark the money.

Media> That's a pity

Gigs> Maybe next time.

Hoops> There's never going to be a next time.

Matthew had been wrong. Never say never he thought. There had been a "next time." It was right now. Matthew had marked his five one-dollar bills before leaving them in the mailbox.

Illustration Credit: Haleigh Lester

Illustration Credit: Haleigh Lester, Lisa Gurack, Kimberly Gurack

See where I've been
Track where I go next!
www.wheresgeorge.com

If the e-mail was a scam, Matthew would be able to track the cybercrook anyway. He would learn the truth, tell all the kids, and be the hero of Rhodes Middle School. Matthew grinned. Life could be sweet.

Gizmo rolled over and whimpered.

"What's the matter?" Matthew whispered.

Gizmo yelped.

"I'm missing something?"

Gizmo shook his head as if he were nodding "yes." Matthew sighed. I'm losing it, he thought. Actually *believing* the dog is saying something to me.

Yet when he closed his eyes, Matthew felt uncomfortable. Instead of images of the kids saying he was the best, Matthew saw flashes of Eddie being bullied by Mike with bystanders looking on.

Then there are the bystanders, Mr. Richie had said softly. They often feel angry and helpless. They don't know what to do but they feel guilty for doing nothing. Sometimes they have nightmares and are haunted by the idea that they'll be the next victims.

A chill ran down Matthew's spine. Why was everything so complicated? He took a deep breath. Tomorrow everything would be different, he told himself.

Matthew fell into a deep sleep. Horrible thoughts crept into his mind . . .

"Where am I?" Matthew screamed suddenly.

"You're in the Oval Office," a man in a dark business suit said. "Listen."

Matthew turned to face the big desk at the end of the room.

"We should trust our fellow Americans. We're all from the same backgrounds."

Matthew stared, bug-eyed, at the President of the United States. Yeah, it was the President, in his suit and tie, sitting at his big desk with the Presidential Seal, the American flag behind him, and a huge pile of fries swimming in mustard in front of him.

"We are a country," the President continued. "America." He smiled.

It was the President, except he had Mr. Richie's face. How did Mr. Richie become President of the United States? Matthew shook his head, trying to clear the confusion.

"It's a nightmare," the President grinned evilly, "and you can't wake up yet."

As if in response to the President's words, Matthew's stomach turned and twisted, and he was spinning away, far away from the oval office . . .

"When in the course of human events, it becomes necessary . . ."

Matthew gawked at Mr. Richie dressed in strange clothes. "Excuse me, uh, Mr. *Jefferson*?" How did Matthew know *his* name?

"Yes, Matthew Hooper?" the President asked.

Kyle leaped into the picture, holding his tiny black tape recorder close to President Jefferson's lips.

"What was the point," Matthew asked hesitantly, "of writing a Declaration of Independence when we're already free?"

"Yes, son, you're right." President-Thomas-Jefferson-with-Mr.-Richie's-face, sighed. "We had to set rules of equality for the future. I wanted to make sure that everyone was treated fairly."

"Does that mean because Eddie is Hispanic, Mike shouldn't beat him up?"

"Yes, Matthew, Eddie is protected by law."

"Oh," Matthew cried.

Once again Matthew felt himself being jerked away, spinning in a swirling darkness, over and over through a strange, sickening void. Then it stopped. The darkness cleared and Matthew was standing in the middle of the school hallway. He took a deep, comforting breath. He was finally on familiar ground!

Matthew peered down the corridor, past the main office and the strangely quiet nurse's office. There was Eddie, calling to him for help. Eddie's cries grew louder, echoing throughout the school. Matthew felt someone pushing against his shoulder. He turned, fear flashing through him. Would it be another President?

It was only Mr. Richie, back in his normal clothes. He was no longer President of the United States, but an ordinary teacher at Rhodes Middle School wearing a silver locket around his neck. Matthew stared at the locket.

"Help him," Mr. Richie demanded.

Matthew started to run in Eddie's direction.

"Yesssssssssss," Mr. Richie cried behind him.

As Matthew ran, Eddie drifted further away. Matthew turned the corner and saw Eddie heading for the stairs. Matthew picked up speed, straining to reach Eddie before he disappeared on the second floor. Matthew glanced at his feet, and there was Gizmo, grinning happily.

"No!" Matthew cried.

Matthew tripped over Gizmo's leash and fell on his face. As hard as he tried, Matthew couldn't untangle himself from the leash. Eddie

Illustration Credit: Sofia-Marie Guttilla

disappeared from view.

Suddenly Mike appeared, laughing loudly. Mr. Richie's voice came over the loudspeaker, reverberating through the building.

"Beware the Ides of March."

"Nooooo," Matthew screamed but the nightmare wouldn't stop.

Matthew felt surrounded by all the kids crowding him, each jamming a tiny black tape recorder into his face. Mike stood in front, hands clenched in fists.

"You're the one who scammed us!" Mike shouted.

They were outside **Burger Blitz**, and Matthew glanced around to see JC, Kyle, Robby, Sara, JC, Alyssa, Jenna, and Breanna encouraging Mike to throw some punches. In the distance, Matthew could see Dylan hiding in the bushes, grinning. Matthew looked in the window of **Burger Blitz** and saw Eddie wiping up a mustard spill.

"Calm down, Mike," Jenna begged. She refused to look at Matthew.

"He took our money, and now he will pay for it!" Mike yelled.

Suddenly there was a crashing sound from the street. Everyone turned. There was the crazy bus driver in his big school bus. It wasn't *exactly* the crazy bus driver, though. It was his bus, his old camouflage fatigues, his new combat boots and . . . *Mr. Richie's face.*

The crazy-bus-driver-with-Mr.-Richie's-face opened the door and started laughing in a creepy, evil tone. Mike's fist moved toward Matthew's head. Suddenly Mike's MP3 player crashed to the pavement, along with Kyle's new shirt, Robby's new backpack, Eddie's new sneakers, Sara's new stereo, Alyssa's new gold chains, JC's new baseball glove, Dylan's new pen, and wads of money floated all around them.

The last thing Matthew saw before Mike's fist came smashing into his face was Breanna's new silver locket.

Matthew's eyes flew open. It was still dark in his room. His heart pounded and his skin was covered with a layer of cold sweat. He glanced at his clock. It was 6:45 A.M. A nightmare had started his day.

The Rhodes Reverie

Monday, March 22

Welcome to the Rhodes Middle School online bulletin board. Post your ideas, thoughts, and adventures! Leave messages for friends and talk about your favorite classes!

>Bus driver gone crazy. Can someone help me?

>Stupido! I win.

>I have a problem. Kids think I'm stupid but I'm not.

>Help! Red Lamborghini stolen! Must have car for my sister.

>Some people are receiving threats or scams on the internet which should be reported.

Chapter Sixteen
Four O'Clock

It should have been one of the best days of the year.

The sun was shining, the air was warm, and there wasn't a cloud in sight. It was the perfect day to hang out with friends, head over to the **Blitz**, or shoot some hoops.

Something very different was happening. Matthew was exhausted from the nightmare.

School was over and as usual, Mike was deciding what they would do. "Hey," he guffawed, "my paper is finally in. Kyle put it all together for me. 90 or above - here I come. Let's celebrate." He raised his arms in a victory salute.

JC glanced at his watch. Sara played with her gold locket. Robby shifted his backpack awkwardly. Alyssa nonchalantly gazed down the block, and Breanna, twisting the chain on her silver locket, stared at Mike. Dan dribbled a basketball, Kyle looked apprehensive, Robby frowned and Jenna shook her head. Matthew could feel the tension in his *bones*.

Suddenly the crazy bus driver revved up his engine and peeled off school grounds laughing maniacally.

What was happening?

Mike sensed it too. "Let's go," he demanded, not smiling.

No one moved.

"Yeah," Robby said finally, "I have to get home. I need to help my brother with his homework no later than 4 o'clock."

Four o'clock? Matthew peered curiously at Robby. It was a strange coincidence. Matthew had to be home by four to check his e-mail for the message from "a friend."

Mike was rankled. "Your brother?"

"Me too," JC added quickly without conviction. "I mean I have to get home to help my mom at the same time. Four o'clock."

"So Dan," Mike grumbled, "are you coming?"

Dan dribbled the basketball. "Same here," he mumbled. "I have to do some computer work."

"I'm going shopping," Sara grinned. "Remember I told you?" she asked Alyssa.

"Me too," Alyssa added quickly, "with my sister."

"You hate your sister," Sara said.

"That's why I'm going shopping with her," Alyssa responded breathlessly. "To make sure she doesn't buy anything that will embarrass me."

Sara narrowed her eyes, clearly doubting Alyssa's reasoning. "That sounds very weird."

Alyssa shrugged.

"What's going on?" Mike persisted. "You're just a bunch of wimps. I could invite Dylan over there, but then again that would be like going by myself in the first place."

Everyone laughed.

Suddenly, all eyes turned to Breanna as she grasped her silver locket.

"What's that?" Sara asked suspiciously.

Breanna frowned.

"It looks just like my locket," Sara continued, "except silver is cheaper."

Breanna shrugged.

"Who gave it to you?" Sara demanded. "It costs too much money for you to pay for it yourself."

Breanna glared at Sara. "It's from my boyfriend."

There was dead silence. Kyle, JC, Mike, Robby, Dan, and Matthew stared at Breanna. They all knew that Breanna didn't have a boyfriend.

"Who's the mystery boyfriend?" Sara asked snidely.

"Maybe it's a secret admirer," Kyle hissed.

"That's none of your business. Anyway, I have to get out of here - you know, I have a doctor's appointment."

"Yeah," Kyle echoed her, "I have a doctor's appointment, too."

"You can't all have doctor appointments," Mike said threateningly.

Jenna grinned. "I have to baby-sit."

"At four?" Sara asked.

Jenna nodded.

"How did I know that?" Sara scowled.

"Matthew?" Mike frowned.

Matthew pretended to be surprised. "You know I have a job puppy sitting. I have to take care of Gizmo."

"What's going on?" Mike asked again. "Everyone can't be busy. The papers are all turned in . . ." He paused. "What is happening at *four*?"

Kyle shrugged.

"Yeah," Mike taunted them, "what are you really doing? Checking your e-mail?"

There was a nail-biting silence that sent an icy chill down Matthew's spine.

"Who told you?" Kyle hissed.

All eyes turned to Kyle.

Mike stared at him quizzically. "Am I missing something here?"

They were silent, waiting for the next shoe to fall.

"What are you talking about?" Matthew asked, the words sticking in his throat.

"Nothing," Kyle said too quickly.

"What are you talking about?" Matthew demanded, unwilling to accept Kyle's response.

Mike shook his head. "This is getting intense."

"No," Jenna whispered nervously, "I don't think it is."

"E-mail," Matthew spat out the word. "What e-mail are you talking about?"

Someone could have put them on a sound stage. The silence was deafening.

"Nothing," Kyle said finally.

"Enough!" Mike railed. "Clue me in."

Everyone ignored him.

"You got the e-mail?" Matthew guessed.

"$5?" Kyle murmured.

"No," Sara and Breanna spoke at the same time. They stared at one another. "You mean you got it too?"

"What is this about?" Mike roared.

No one heard him.

"Who else?" Matthew asked hoarsely. He went from face to face. They didn't have to say anything.

They had all received the same e-mail: $5 to find out the name of the cybercrook and a guarantee they would get their $30 back.

"I don't understand," Matthew said thickly. "It was addressed to *me*."

"No it wasn't," Jenna jumped in hastily. "It was addressed to me."

Matthew turned on her. "*Why you?* You didn't even buy a paper."

Jenna paled. "I thought . . . I . . . I mean, I believed I would solve everything and get the money back for everyone else."

"I want to know what's going on," Mike bellowed, pushing his way into the middle of the group.

Mike always has to be the center of attention, Matthew thought. He has to control everything.

Matthew glared at Mike. "Don't you know?"

"Know what?"

"About the e-mail. Didn't you get the e-mail?"

"I don't know what you're talking about."

"Didn't you get the e-mail offering the identity of the cybercrook for $5?"

It was the first time that Matthew saw Mike falter. Mike's shoulders drooped, his eyes were uncertain, and his fingers fluttered nervously.

"I didn't get any e-mail," Mike said defensively.

"Is there anyone else," Matthew scanned the group, "who *didn't* get the e-mail?"

Everyone was speechless.

"We were scammed again," Matthew said sharply. "We were all scammed again

except . . . Mike."

All eyes fixed accusingly on Mike.

"Why did everyone get the e-mail but you?" Matthew asked evenly.

For the first time Mike had no answer.

"Maybe Mike scammed us." JC's voice was harsh.

"Yeah," Jenna agreed. "He has a new MP3 player. That costs hundreds of dollars."

"He would have had enough money to buy ten MP3 players," JC mumbled.

"With money left over," Robby grunted.

"He's so *used* to having money that he'll try to get more at any cost," Alyssa frowned.

"Leave him alone," Sara cried.

"He probably didn't even get the chance to check his e-mail," Breanna added defensively.

"Think about it guys," JC said, "Mike turned his paper in late. What a great decoy."

"Wait," Mike shouted, struggling to regain control. "Why would I steal money from you?"

"He's right." Kyle agreed. "Why would Mike steal the papers only to turn in his late?"

Matthew stared at JC. Shifting the blame to Mike would be a great way for JC to throw the kids off *his* trail if he were the cybercrook. Matthew struggled to recall whether JC had been spending a lot of money recently.

"Chill out guys." Mike said desperately. "You all got scammed again; you're trying to blame it on me. Be real. Eddie wouldn't hesitate to scam you out of more money - but he wouldn't do anything to *me*. He's too scared."

No one responded.

"Don't you see?" Mike was like a soldier plunging into battle. "Eddie wants everyone to believe that I did it. That way he'll get me off his back *and* keep *all the money*. I mean, all the money. Now it's $35 from each of you." Mike thrust out his chest and deepened his voice. "He did it *again*."

Matthew was in awe. The kids looked uncertain, shifting their feet and looking away from one another.

Mike went in for the kill. "Freaking Eddie made fools of us. Don't you see that?"

Suddenly Dylan joined the conversation. "Mike's right," he said succinctly. "Eddie is your man." He turned and left the group. It was several minutes before anyone spoke.

Kyle was the first. "Yeah, you're right. Eddie scammed us again."

"Boy were we *stupid*," Sara grumbled, "paying out another five bucks."

"Stupid is not the word," Breanna shivered.

"I really thought that I was the only one getting the e-mail. It was addressed to me and . . ." Robby sighed.

Matthew hung his head. "Me too. He even said to put the money under the door mat."

"I don't have a door mat," Sara said, "so he told me to put it in the mailbox."

"He told me to leave it under a rock by the tree in front of my house," JC volunteered.

Each one had a slightly different version.

"He customized it," Dan said.

"Which means," Kyle offered, "that he knows each one of us."

They were quiet thinking about the implications of Kyle's comment.

He knows each one of us.

Matthew shivered.

"We have to stop this guy," Robby said, "once and for all."

"Now you're talking," Mike prodded them on.

"He's really messing with us," JC raised his voice. "I don't want it to happen again."

"It can't happen again," Dan said.

"Wait," Matthew intervened. "Dan, I thought you wrote your own paper like Jenna."

"I did," Dan said defiantly.

"Then why did you get the e-mail too?"

"Beats me," Dan smiled sheepishly.

"He's the computer nerd," Sara interjected. "If he found the truth and got our money back, we would think he's the best."

Dan shrugged. "It was *only* five bucks. I didn't think I could lose."

Matthew shook his head. "You lost just like the rest of us."

"Eddie is so freaking smart," Mike bellowed. "He even got Dan into this mess."

"You got it right Mike."

"Yeah, Mike, you see the real thing."

"Freaking Eddie - we have to get him."

"We have to get our money back."

"He deserves to get really messed up."

"Yeah, let's mess up Eddie."

Matthew backed away. The voices blurred into a verbal assault.

"Yeah, we'll mess Eddie up until we get our money back, and then go back for more just to show who's boss."

"Yeah."

"We'll get the slime."

"No doubt."

It was getting ugly. Matthew didn't know what would happen next. He thought of Morf's words.

The situation might get much worse before it gets better.

The voices continued.

"Teach him a real lesson."

"He'll know what we're made of."

"*Latino boy*."

"Freaking *Latino boy*."

"We'll show him that no Latino boy can come into our neighborhood and . . ."

Matthew didn't know what to do. How could he stop them? Didn't they see where all of this was headed? Without realizing what was happening, Matthew imagined himself back in Mr. Richie's class.

There's something called collective behavior . . . When you trade in your "self" for the identity of the crowd and become more suggestible this strange feeling of power emerges. Suddenly you feel invincible.

Something very evil was taking form. Matthew had no idea what to do next. Instead, Matthew ran.

Illustration Credit: Mike Monteverde

Chapter Seventeen
The Final Straw

He hated to run away, but Matthew couldn't help himself.

Matthew raced down the street, his backpack slamming against him, his breath coming in quick, rapid gasps and his chest burning from the exertion. He didn't have any answers so he ran away from the group.

Matthew's group had become cruel, malicious, and determined to hurt Eddie. Now they were dangerous, exactly as Mr. Richie had warned. If Matthew sided with Eddie, he would lose his group. Matthew's friends would hate him. He knew what that felt like; it was unbearable to even think about it. On the other hand, if Matthew sided with his group he would break the pact with Eddie. He would leave Eddie alone, unprotected, and unable to figure out the truth. If Eddie was innocent . . . Matthew simply couldn't stand the idea of supporting people who were convicting an innocent guy. Matthew had been there before, too. If he tried to play the middle, everyone would be angry with him - he wouldn't have his group *or* Eddie.

Matthew took a deep breath. He had to think it through very carefully. Checking his e-mail would be his next step. As soon as he was logged on, Matthew saw the message from "a friend." He clicked on the e-mail.

```
To: Matthew
From: A friend
Subject: Your money
Date: Monday, March 22

Hi Matthew.


Scammed Again!

You're a great target - thanks 4 the pocket
money :-)
```

Matthew saw red.

He didn't think he could be so angry, but the rage bubbled up like a pot of boiling water. He had been so stupid . . . so *ignorant* to believe that he had fallen for a scam the second time.

Matthew screamed out loud, his voice scraping his throat, making it feel raw and vulnerable. His hands trembled with fury, and his heart pounded. All he wanted to do was to hit someone, strike out at . . . Eddie?

Matthew stared at his fists.

He wanted to grab Eddie by his shoulders, pummel his face, shove him against the wall just like in the movies and demand that every penny . . .

Eddie?

Matthew struggled to contain his wrath. Were those Mike's thoughts or his own? Was he thinking like the crowd? Matthew walked into both scams knowing exactly what he was doing. Why was he so furious? Why was he now so willing to blame Eddie?

So I don't have to blame myself.

Matthew shivered. There wouldn't have been any scam without his or his friends' participation. The thought cut through him like a knife tearing up his insides.

So I don't have to blame myself.

Matthew was so immersed in his inner war that he hardly heard Gizmo's wild barking.

So I don't have to blame myself.

Gizmo burst into his room, barked loudly and tore downstairs. Was it time to walk Gizmo again? Matthew took a deep breath. Maybe paying some attention to the dog would take his mind away from what was happening at school.

Matthew followed Gizmo downstairs, ignoring his barking. He located the leash and snapped it onto Gizmo's collar.

"Let's go," Matthew grumbled.

Gizmo yanked him toward the door.

"Easy," Matthew commanded.

The puppy didn't care.

Shaking his head, Matthew opened the door and was dragged outside. He could see that Nicole was shooting hoops all by herself, across the street in the driveway. Matthew barely had the chance to close the door before Gizmo dragged him over to Nicole.

"Yeah," Matthew grumbled, "you must *really* need to go out."

"Gizmo," Nicole called, kneeling down and opening her arms.

She's more interested in the dog than me, Matthew thought. He added that to his list of troubles.

Gizmo leaped at Nicole, covering her faces with wet, doggy kisses. Matthew couldn't help but laugh; it was such a crazy sight. Nicole fell back, onto the pavement, laughing along with Matthew.

Yeah, Matthew did feel better. He relaxed a bit. Gizmo had a way of doing that.

The feeling didn't last long.

From the corner of his eye he saw Jenna running down the block. Wasn't Jenna supposed to be with the kids? He was overcome with the feeling that something very bad was happening.

Nicole and Gizmo looked up from pavement. Gizmo stopped licking her.

All three waited as Jenna raced wildly down the block.

Jenna finally arrived, her eyes were wild looking and her lips trembling as she gasped for breath. "Matthew hurry," she cried.

"What are you talking about?"

"*Quick*," her voice was thick with fear. Gizmo pulled away from Nicole, barking and nipping at Jenna's ankles. It was the first time that Matthew had seen the puppy not like someone.

"What's going on?" Matthew asked with urgency.

"We can't talk. We have to get there now."

"Where?"

Jenna stumbled over the words, barely making sense.

Matthew pulled Gizmo away. "Hang on to this," he handed the leash to Nicole. Gizmo leaned against Nicole's legs and stared unhappily at Jenna.

"Stay calm, Jenna. Tell me what's going on?"

"After you left everyone got really mad, I mean," Jenna gulped, "*furious*."

"Yeah?"

"So Mike said it's time to take care of Eddie once and for all. Everyone agreed - or at least, followed him."

"What?"

Jenna nodded. "They all took off for the **Burger Blitz** saying it was time Eddie got his due. I followed them there. They're looking to beat him up, Matthew. They're so mad . . . well, anything can happen. They can rip into his face," tears started streaming down her face, "and it's all my fault."

"Your fault?"

"I tried to stop them. I really did," Jenna said quickly. "But they didn't listen. They were so angry about the money and the scams, that they didn't listen. They ignored me."

"I don't understand."

"Don't you see," she screamed, "it's not Eddie."

"How do you know that?"

Jenna was suddenly silent. She stared at him warily. "I mean, I *think* it's not Eddie. You know, I believe it's not Eddie." She stumbled over her words. "Oh that doesn't matter right now anyway because Eddie is going to get hurt unless we stop them."

"We?"

"You and I, Matthew. We have to stop them before this gets worse."

Jenna? Matthew thought. Why would a girl be a cybercrook?

Matthew remembered Jenna's story in English class. Her dad had lost his job after the terrorist attacks on September 11. Jenna had to baby-sit to make money - she couldn't even afford to buy a paper. Matthew shook his head in frustration. How could he possibly suspect Jenna when she had been so helpful? He had to focus in on the moment and concentrate on what was happening at the **Blitz**.

"Stop thinking," Jenna wailed. "Just come with me!"

Matthew glanced at Nicole. "Can you watch Gizmo for me?"

"Yeah," she said uncertainly. "Are you sure you want to do this?"

"I have to."

"Okay, Matthew. Just be careful."

Matthew nodded. "This is the fastest way," he turned to Jenna.

They took the shortcut through the Doyle's backyard. Buddy, the Doyle's big, affectionate Dalmatian, ran to greet them. Matthew paused, allowing Buddy to sniff. Suddenly a warm, doggy tongue was licking his hand and staring uncertainly at Jenna.

Interesting, Matthew thought. Dogs don't like Jenna.

"C'mon," Jenna cried, "we don't have time."

Matthew nodded, gave Buddy one last pat, and crossed through the yard. Within minutes, they were at the **Blitz**. Matthew stared through the front window. A large group of kids had crowded around the counter. They were all the kids that had been talking about Eddie at school - JC, Sara, Kyle, Dan, Alyssa, Breanna, Robby, with, of course, Mike in the lead. Other kids had shown up to see what was going on. Matthew recognized a lot of faces from Mr. Richie's other classes. He could feel the tension before he even entered the **Blitz**.

Mr. Richie's words came back.

People go out to protest or celebrate or just watch - it doesn't really matter. They lose themselves in the identity of the crowd, get a feeling of power and then are easily led into dangerous behaviors. In the old west they hung people from trees using the "lynching mob" mentality. Today, people loot stores, attack police, and do all sorts of crazy things.

Matthew shivered. He and Jenna went into the **Blitz**. They plunged into the crowd, pushing their way toward the front. Many of the kids held dollar bills in their hands, waving them like flags as if to demand their money be returned.

Mike's livid voice pierced Matthew's ears, filling the air with a collective rage.

"You *did* it again," Mike fumed. "Stole another five bucks. Do you think we're that stupid, Blitz?"

All faces were focused on Mike. The kids mirrored one another - eyes fiery, teeth bared, and jaws clenched. Led by Mike, it felt like the kids blended into one voice with one intentional target.

"I'm going to take you out," Mike railed, "unless you give me back my money."

A roar went up from the crowd. More dollar bills were waved threateningly in the air.

"*Moneyyyyyyy. Moneyyyyyyy,*" the crowd chanted.

Matthew pushed harder, elbowing people in front of him. He lost Jenna - she was too small to break through the angry pack.

"You're just a cheap, lying rip," Mike roared.

Matthew was getting closer to the front.

"I'm going to beat that freaking face to a pulp. You'll remember me for the rest of your life, *Latino boy*."

Matthew used all his strength to break through the line of boys immediately surrounding Mike. They didn't want to let him in - he felt the tense concentration in their bodies like cats ready to lunge.

"See this fist," Mike bellowed.

Only Kyle was between Matthew and Mike.

Matthew shoved him hard. Kyle turned to see what was happening. His eyes were glassy. Instead of waving a dollar bill like the other kids, Kyle held the tiny black box in his hand.

"Kyle," Matthew cried, "what are you doing?"

Kyle didn't answer. Instead, he turned, thrusting the box in front of Mike's face.

Suddenly Matthew realized what Kyle was doing.

He was Editor-in-Chief of *The Rhodes Reporter*. Kyle was *tape recording* the story.

Matthew felt dizzy. Was that all Kyle cared about?

How he could write a good story for the school newspaper?

Matthew pushed his way in front of Kyle and froze.

Eddie stood behind the counter, his eyes filled with terror. He had shrunk away from Mike, cowering against the cash register. The draw to the register was open and Eddie had a fist of money in his hand as if he had been frozen in the process of making change. Mike edged closer, his voice spewing curses.

Matthew turned back to the crowd. They were alive with waving bills, lost in a sea of money and maniacal chants.

Then Matthew saw it in the crowd - a one-dollar bill. Written across the front in a clear red marker in Matthew's own handwriting was:

See where I've been
Track where I go next!
www.wheresgeorge.com

The cybercrook was among them.

Matthew frantically searched the crowd. Who was it? There were so many people watching, mumbling, tensing for battle, and waving their dollar bills.

"This fist is going down your throat," Mike hollered.

"Yeah," people in the crowd echoed Mike.

"Yeah," Mike yelled.

Matthew's heart pounded out of control. He was desperate to figure out who was waving the marked bill.

"Get him," the crowd roared, blocking Matthew's view.

Eddie was terrified. Was it plain fear or was it guilt? Matthew could

Illustration Credit: Lauren Williams

smell Eddie's fear.

"Rip him apart," the crowd demanded.

Mike raised his fist.

Matthew desperately searched the crowd. The marked bill disappeared and then reappeared. Although he was tall, Matthew still couldn't connect the bill to a person. He had to find out who was waving it. All the answers were so close and yet so far . . .

"Give him what he deserves," the crowd rose as in one voice. "Kill."

Matthew was suddenly driven in a direction he couldn't comprehend. It could be Mike, Eddie, Kyle, Robby, JC, Alyssa, Sara, Breanna or anyone else holding that bill. While the crowd screamed for blood, the cybercrook was lurking secretly in their midst. He or she was part of this frenzy, an integral piece of the puzzle.

"Blood," the crowd cheered.

They had to be stopped before Eddie was seriously hurt. But how? On the fringes, Matthew saw Jenna waving frantically at him. "Stop it," she mouthed hysterically.

Someone had to break the onslaught.

Matthew raised his arms high and screamed, as loud as he could, "Stop!"

No one heard him.

Matthew screamed again. "Stop!"

"Blood," the crowd roared louder.

"Stop," Matthew shrieked again and again until his throat was raw and dry.

The crowd could not be stopped.

"Blood," Mike swung his fist at Eddie.

"Blood," the crowd exploded in delight.

Mike's fist hit Eddie's face. Matthew could actually hear the smash of bone against flesh above the deafening cheers of the crowd. Abruptly, everything shifted into slow motion. Eddie fell back against the force of Mike's fist, Mike raised his arms in triumph, and the blood spewed from Eddie's nose like ketchup boiling over its plastic squirt bottle.

Matthew heard sirens and looked over his shoulder to see a police car racing down the street. With all his strength, Matthew squeezed himself closer to the counter and yelled at Eddie. "Run," Matthew hissed, "I'll meet you at Nicole's."

Eddie had covered his nose with his fingers, trying to stop the bleeding. His eyes widened as he grasped Matthew's message.

"Run," Matthew repeated as the cops entered the **Blitz**. "*Now*."

The crowd shifted to face the police.

"What's going on here?" the officer demanded.

It was another voice - a distraction to break the melee. The crowd began to deteriorate, just as Mr. Richie had described. Mike slunk into oblivion behind Kyle, Jenna collapsed on a chair in the corner, and

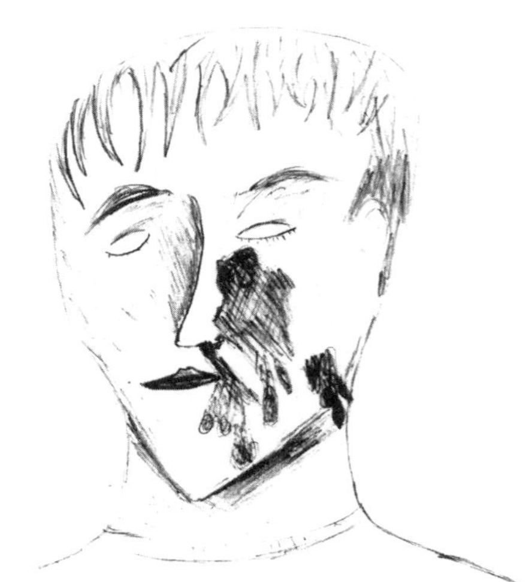

Illustration Credit: Bryan Brown

Matthew made his way toward the emergency exit next to the bathroom. He took one final look at the crowd. Many of the kids had stopped waving the money. The Wheresgeorge.com bill was still in the air. In one final struggle, Matthew moved from the emergency exit and broke into the center of the crowd, following the bill.

"What's going on here?" The officer bellowed.

Then everything became crystal clear.

Matthew knew immediately who held the marked money.

He broke from the crowd, the visions of mustard and silver lockets floating through his head as if he were thrown back to his awful nightmare.

"What's going on here," two more police yelled as they pushed their way into the **Burger Blitz**.

Illustration Credit: Mike Monteverde

Chapter Eighteen
Show Me The Money

Matthew staggered home, shocked by what he had seen.

Mike had viciously attacked Eddie. The mob had mindlessly supported Mike. They were all wrong. The cybercrook was there, but it wasn't Eddie *or* Mike.

Matthew had caught the cybercrook red-handed. He almost hated knowing the truth. Matthew realized that knowing the identity of the cybercrook was nearly as bad as *not* knowing. He just didn't want to believe it was *her* - the victim of another Rhodes Middle School bully.

By the time Matthew arrived at Nicole's house, he looked almost as beaten up as Eddie.

Gizmo jumped on him, and Nicole asked, with apparent concern. "Are you okay Matthew? You look awful."

Matthew could only stare at her.

"What happened?"

Gizmo sat obediently at Matthew's feet, as if he were waiting for the answer, too.

"I know who did it," Matthew said weakly. "It makes me feel terrible."

"Are you sure?"

Matthew nodded.

"How did you find out?"

"It was the money. This time I marked it."

"This time?"

"Yeah," Matthew grinned sheepishly. "Yesterday, the cybercrook scammed us for another $5. This time I marked the bills, like you suggested. I just saw someone at the *Blitz* holding one of the bills . . ."

"It would be worth five bucks," Nicole said smugly, "to catch the cybercrook."

"Yeah," Matthew agreed weakly. "I guess."

"How do you know you have the right person?"

"The marked bills were picked up this morning. They didn't have any time to be put in circulation before school and . . ." Matthew shrugged.

"I get it. Who is the cybercrookt?"

Matthew whispered the name.

"Who? I couldn't hear you."

"Breanna," Matthew said loudly and painfully. "Breanna is the cybercrook."

Nicole took a step back. "I don't believe it!"

"I guess it makes sense in a strange sort of way," Matthew rubbed Gizmo's long, floppy ears.

"I don't understand."

"Well, you know about her sister always getting in trouble?"

"Yeah, I heard the stories. She's not the kid that got kicked out of RCC?"

"Nah. That *would* make a good story, though."

They laughed half-heartedly.

"Maybe she needed bail money for her sister," Matthew offered.

"C'mon. Breanna's sister is not *that* bad."

Matthew shrugged.

"What else?"

"Well," Matthew said slowly, " Sara is always picking on Breanna and Breanna really likes Mike. So maybe it's a way to get back at Sara."

"Aren't there better ways?"

"I guess. Then there's the silver locket."

"The silver locket?"

"Yeah, suddenly Breanna appears with a silver locket, similar to the one that Mike gave Sara. Breanna doesn't have extra money for a locket. She says it's from her boyfriend, but we all know Breanna doesn't *have* a boyfriend. Sara calls him the mystery boyfriend."

"I don't know," Nicole said doubtfully. "It's so *circumstantial*."

"I don't like it either. Breanna had the marked dollar bills, so she has to be the cybercrook. Sara bullies Breanna all the time. Mr. Richie said that victims of bullies can turn dangerous when they try to seek revenge."

Nicole was about to respond. Instead, her eyes widened, and she covered her mouth with her hand. Matthew followed her gaze.

Eddie was hobbling down the block, clearly moving with great difficulty.

No one moved.

Eddie slowly approached them.

Gizmo stiffened.

"Hey man," Matthew said softly, "are you ok?"

It was obvious that Eddie wasn't okay. His face was speckled with dried blood, his top lip was swollen, and a large, purple bruise spread from his nose across his cheek. Nicole touched his arm gently.

"Let me get you some ice," she said softly.

Eddie shook his head.

"That was one of the ugliest things I've ever seen," Matthew said stiffly.

"Yeah," Eddie spoke as if his mouth was filled with food. Matthew figured that Eddie's cheek was even more swollen *inside*. "Mike gave it to me."

"What happened after I left?"

Eddie took a deep breath. "The cops started to clear the place, so I just ran before anyone could stop me. I was afraid," his eyes glistened with tears, "of what could happen next."

"I don't blame you," Matthew agreed. "You didn't deserve it."

"You're right I didn't deserve it," Eddie said bitterly. "No one wants to believe me."

"I do," Jenna interjected. No one had noticed her jogging down the street.

"Thanks," Eddie mumbled.

Nicole grabbed Jenna's hand. "He didn't do it, you know. He's innocent."

Eddie stared at Nicole.

"We know," Matthew said slowly, "who the cybercrook is."

"Who?" Eddie growled. "I'm going to kill that guy."

"It's not a guy."

Jenna glanced at Matthew strangely. "It's not a guy?"

"No."

"A girl?"

"Yeah."

"Who," Eddie's voice was weaker. "Which girl hates me that much?"

"Breanna," Matthew said stiffly and then explained his reasoning.

"I can't believe it Breanna did this," Jenna scowled. "She just doesn't have enough reason to do it."

Eddie shook his head painfully. "Why does Breanna *hate* me? What did I ever do to her?"

Matthew shrugged.

"It just doesn't make sense," Nicole mumbled.

Gizmo barked.

They all turned to see what Gizmo was barking at. Matthew's heart began to pound. Gizmo barked again, much louder. Matthew wanted desperately to run. He was afraid he couldn't stop what was about to happen.

A mob was coming down the street. They moved in step with one another, the tension floating above them like a storm cloud, their hands waving dollar bills like flags, chanting in one eerie, terrifying voice.

"Moneyyyyyyy. Moneyyyyyyy."

Mike was out in front with muscles rippling like evil weapons, his eyes blazing, and his mouth set in a snarl as if ready to pounce. Kyle was prancing next to Mike, alternately thrusting his tiny black tape recorder between Mike and the crowd. Sara was close behind and . . . the others moved as one, readying for the kill: JC, Breanna, Alyssa, Robby and other kids from school, all caught up in the craziness. Even Dylan was with them, stepping to the same rhythm as the others.

A lynching mob.

Matthew prayed for Mr. Richie to suddenly appear and diffuse the mob. He knew it was impossible. Matthew knew the truth. It was up to him to break down the collective behavior and get them to think like individuals again.

"Help me Gizmo," Matthew whispered, touching the dog's head. "Please help me."

Gizmo stiffened until he looked like he was standing at attention.

It was only minutes before Mike was upon them.

Matthew, Jenna, and Nicole stood in front of Eddie, protecting him with their bodies.

"Move away," Mike demanded.

The kids circled, chanting and urging Mike on.

Out of the corner of his eye, Matthew saw Kyle toss his half-zipped backpack on the sidewalk so he could leap around the kids and record everything they said.

I can't believe it, Matthew thought again. *All he cares about is the story*.

"I'm going to kill that Latino," Mike hissed.

"No, you're not," Matthew forced his voice to be calm.

"The cops came too quickly at the **Blitz**," Mike continued, "but they're not here now. He made fools of all of us." Mike swept a meaty arm over the mob. "He's going down for that."

"Yeahhhhhhhhhhhhhhhh."

The crowd shouted.

"Killlllllllllllllllllllllllllll."

The crowd chanted.

"Moneyyyyyyyyyyyyyyyyy."

The crowd demanded.

"You have the wrong person," Matthew screamed above the melee. "I can prove it." Suddenly a tiny black box was thrust in front of his face. It was the tape recorder. Angrily, Matthew pushed Kyle away. "It's not Eddie. I can prove it."

There was a tiny pause in the action - an entry way into the collective madness that held his friends prisoners.

"No way," someone raised his voice above the others.

"NoWayyyyyyyyyyyyyyyyyyyyy."

The crowd reverberated.

Mike stretched his body taller, and waved his fists. "If you don't let me through to the cybercrook, Hooper, I'll smash you first."

Matthew stared at Mike's fist. He was terrified. All trails led to Breanna.

"It's Breanna," Matthew screamed. "She's the cybercrook."

There was instant silence.

The crowd parted slightly to allow Breanna to face Matthew. Kyle dodged into the hole, so he could catch Breanna's response.

"Me?" Her voice was confused rather than afraid.

It wasn't the voice of a criminal who has suddenly been caught red-handed.

"You, Breanna," Matthew said as fiercely as he could. "I have proof."

Breanna froze. "What are you talking about? Is this some kind of joke?"

The kids slowly moved away from her.

Mike stared too, not knowing what to say.

Matthew took one of the biggest risks of his life. He stepped away from his back up, allowing Jenna, Nicole, and Eddie to face the crowd of hostile kids.

"First," Matthew reached over and grabbed the dollar bill from her hand. "How did you get this?"

"What are you talking about?" Breanna's voice was thick with fear.

"I marked the bills I left for the cybercrook this morning." Matthew took a deep breath. "You're the only one who has one. See the wheresgeorge.com written in red ink?"

Several kids glanced at the dollar bills they were holding in their hands. The silence was agonizing.

"I . . ." Breanna began, "I borrowed it for my lunch and . . ."

Matthew cut her off. "Where did you get the money to pay for the silver locket?" He raised his voice. "Where?"

Breanna grabbed the locket in her hand. "It was a gift," she said weakly. "I didn't pay for it."

"From who?"

"My boyfriend."

"We all know you don't have a boyfriend."

Breanna's cheeks reddened. "I . . ."

"We know the truth," Matthew raised his arms in the air. "You bought it with the money you got from selling us the papers."

"Noooooooooo," Breanna cried. "Someone gave it to me. I don't know who . . . I just wore it because Sara . . ." Matthew knew Sara's locket held a tiny picture of Mike. Breanna slipped the locket over her head and thrust it at Matthew. "Look."

Matthew flipped open the locket. There was no picture inside Breanna's silver locket, only a few words scrawled on a tiny paper.

Kyle jammed the recorder in Matthew's face.

"Read it," Breanna wailed hysterically. "Read it."

Matthew peered at the words. He read them out loud slowly. "From a secret admirer."

There was a frozen silence as the kids struggled to digest what had happened.

Matthew was sweating profusely. All the trails seem to lead directly to Breanna. Maybe he was wrong, maybe Breanna wasn't the cybercrook . . .

Without thinking, he dropped Gizmo's leash. No one noticed.

Maybe Breanna had gotten hold of the marked bill in another way? Maybe someone could have passed it in the school cafeteria or even at the **Blitz**, before everything heated up?

I can't believe it was Breanna, Jenna had said. *She just doesn't have enough reason to do it.*

Maybe Matthew was wrong and Eddie and . . .

He didn't have time to complete the thought. Gizmo started barking passionately. Everyone turned to look at the curly-haired puppy. Gizmo had dashed away from the crowd and before anyone could stop him, lunged for a half-zipped black backpack on the sidewalk.

"Shut it," Matthew cried at Gizmo.

Gizmo didn't listen. He grabbed the backpack in his teeth and swung his head back and forth, over and over again, with all his puppy strength.

"Stop it," Matthew cried. He took one step forward and then froze.

All eyes were on Gizmo.

Wads of money were flying out from the backpack.

No one moved.

Suddenly, Gizmo dropped the backpack, picked up something in his teeth and trotted over to Matthew.

"What's that," Matthew asked incredulously.

Gizmo offered his prize.

It was a floppy disk.

"That's my missing disk," Eddie whispered.

Gizmo sat at Matthew's feet, a doggy smile spreading across his face.

"My backpack!" Kyle howled. "What did that dog *do* to my backpack?" Kyle broke from the crowd. He frantically grabbed the backpack, stuffing the wads of money back inside.

There was a crashing sound on the pavement.

Matthew, Gizmo, and all the kids stared.

Kyle's tiny black tape recorder had fallen to the sidewalk, smashing into a thousand tiny pieces.

Illustration Credit: Jordan Schneider

The Rhodes Reporter

Cybercrook Confesses to Internet Scam

By Eddie Pizarro

In a drama that shocked the entire Rhodes community, ex-Editor-in-Chief of The Rhodes Reporter confessed to masterminding the research paper scam!

It began when Kyle's first cousin, Steven Norton, was expelled for plagiarism from Rhodes Community College. Infuriated, Kyle Harris claimed it was a terrible injustice and vowed revenge.

Dr. Manuel Pizarro, was the RCC professor responsible for the expulsion. When his son, me, Eddie Pizarro, walked into The Rhodes Reporter office, Kyle seized his opportunity to use the son to get back at the father. Kyle stole the disk where I stored my paper and my article for The Rhodes Reporter. He knew it was there because when I copied it to the newspaper database, Kyle was looking over my shoulder.

The rest was easy. Kyle had kids' e-mail addresses because he was Editor-in-Chief. Most of the kids in Mr. Richie's class fell for the scam. When he posted the warning on Rhodes Reverie, everyone had to work really hard to quickly write a paper. The kids were furious! Since I wrote the paper, everyone figured I was the cybercrook. Big Mike led the mob, determined to get the money back or kill me.

It was the mustard that gave him away. Breanna Wills was the only other kid who used mustard on hamburger and fries. Kyle liked her, but knew that she wanted Mike. In hopes of winning her, Kyle used the scam money to buy a silver locket for Breanna. He included the message, "from your secret admirer."
You know the rest.

Kyle gave the list of kids who bought papers, to Mr. Richie. Those kids were punished for "intent to plagiarize." They had the choice of writing a 10-page paper on plagiarism or bullying, and perform 20 hours of community service. Instead of returning their money, Mr. Richie donated it to the National Education Association's National Bullying Awareness Campaign.

Kyle was punished the most severely. He had to write an apology to the students, Mr. Richie, Eddie, and Dr. Pizarro for his criminal behavior. He was suspended from school for the remainder of the year and permanently removed from his position as Editor-in-Chief. All scam money was given to Mr. Richie (who donated it). Lastly, Kyle was sentenced to 200 hours of community service.

Need advice on where to do your community service?

(working with the Crazy Bus Driver doesn't count!)

Contact Mr. Richie

The Rhodes Reverie

Monday, April 6

Welcome to the Rhodes Middle School online bulletin board. Post your ideas, thoughts, and adventures! Leave messages for friends and talk about your favorite classes!

>My left shoe is still missing!

>Congratulations to our new RHODES REPORTER Editor-in-Chief, Eddie Pizarro.

>Purchased brown cow with white and black spots. Looking for another cow, yellow with brown spots. Any available?

>Lost black purse - contains a manuscript called Matthew's Tangled Trails, calculator, mirror, pens and pencils

>Looking for the person who broke the window at Lindsay's party.

>Dog found on the streets of Philadelphia. Please claim.

>Help! Stolen sister! Must have Red Lamborghini for her ransom.

The Making of Matthew's Tangled Trails

Illustration Credit: Rebecca Vedrin and Dalla Gaon

Table of Contents

Illustration Credit: Cesar Gonzalez

The Making of Matthew's Tangled Trails

The deliberations had begun! It was time to decide *who did it*? and the Merrick Avenue Middle School authors were at it again. Everyone had an opinion and an equal say in the outcome. It was more like Presidential candidates battling it out in a debate on national television than teenagers collaborating on a Young Adult Mystery.

That's the way it was from the very first page. The teenagers from Mrs. Ellen Schwartz's 7th grade Honors classes took their jobs very seriously. They were determined to make their book top notch, from content to grammar, and eagerly voiced their opinions. "I have found some things I think should be re-thought," one student, Mike Monteverde, e-mailed. "The book has a more serious vibe and some characters, like the crazy bus driver, although funny, should be removed." Cesar Gonzalez wrote, "I don't think the book should call people with a Spanish background, Latinos. To some people that term is offensive."

The student authors made their positions clear. Brian Tannenbaum, Landon Marder, Lindsay Melworm, and Amanda Burnett expressed their concerns by observing, "we think that the kids on the web should be mentioned more, Nicole should have a screen name, and that it's very weird that Gigs can memorize the RAMS website. Also, the words, "they squared their shoulders" is mentioned way too much."

Often, disagreements had to be solved with basic democratic process - class votes. Sean Keegan requested that Breanna be spelled with an "e" rather than an "i" because "my sister's name is Breanna. Could you please change the spelling for sentimental reasons? It would be a great surprise for Breanna when I show her." It was resolved in a majority vote. Similarly, choosing the cybercrook required three votes, using both the process of elimination and ultimately, compromise.

The kids were extraordinary - enthusiastic, hard working, and committed. Ideas and words flowed like moves in a video game, full of energy and determination. Everyone was an active participant. For example, to compose Matthew's nightmare, three groups of kids directly contributed to the content: The D.A.L.J.S. (Danielle Schwarz, Andrew Bank, Lisa Gurock, Jordan Wolfson, and Shaun Werbelow); The HKKIMD (Hailey Simon, Kim Gurock, Kelly McCarthy, Ian Li, Doug Gibbons, and Michael George); and The Dodo Birds + A Girl (Michelle Kremer, Zach Coppola, Matt Cohen, and Mitchell Kochman). All of the students wrote posts for *The Rhodes Reverie*, articles or statements to *The Rhodes Reporter*, bully stories, and an assortment of ideas, stories, and writing that molded *Matthew's Tangled Trails* into a very special book. The following pages tell *their* story.

Illustration Credit: Jordan Schneider

A Message from Merrick Avenue Middle School

The greatest gift an English teacher can bestow is to teach his or her students this noble truth: that the process of reading is one of the most enjoyable activities open to us as human beings. Academic success, existential knowledge, fulfilling employment (even better SAT scores!) can all derive from this simple understanding. Sadly, this is a difficult task, and one of the most challenging hurdles is the search for books that are both entertaining and meaningful. What great works of young adult literature have in common is their ability to truly communicate to children of a specific age: to speak to them in the voice of their own hearts. By initiating this collaboration between two adult authors and a group of seventh grade children, Jeri Fink, Donna Paltrowitz, and Ellen Schwartz have succeeded in a plethora of arenas rarely open to educators, parents, or writers. The authors have heard first hand the dreams and fears of the children about whom they write; the teacher has given her students the chance to learn about writing and about language by doing, not merely observing; and our students have had the opportunity to be listened to, to be respected, and to take part in an act of creation beyond what any of them might accomplish individually. The fact that this novel is also providing a forum for kids to talk honestly about the contemporary problems they face is an unexpected reward. We are extremely proud of the parents, teachers, and students who made this book possible. This is a truly innovative learning experience which all of the parties will be sure to remember for years to come.

Ms. Caryn Frange
Ms. Teresa Grossane
Mr. Sean Llewellyn

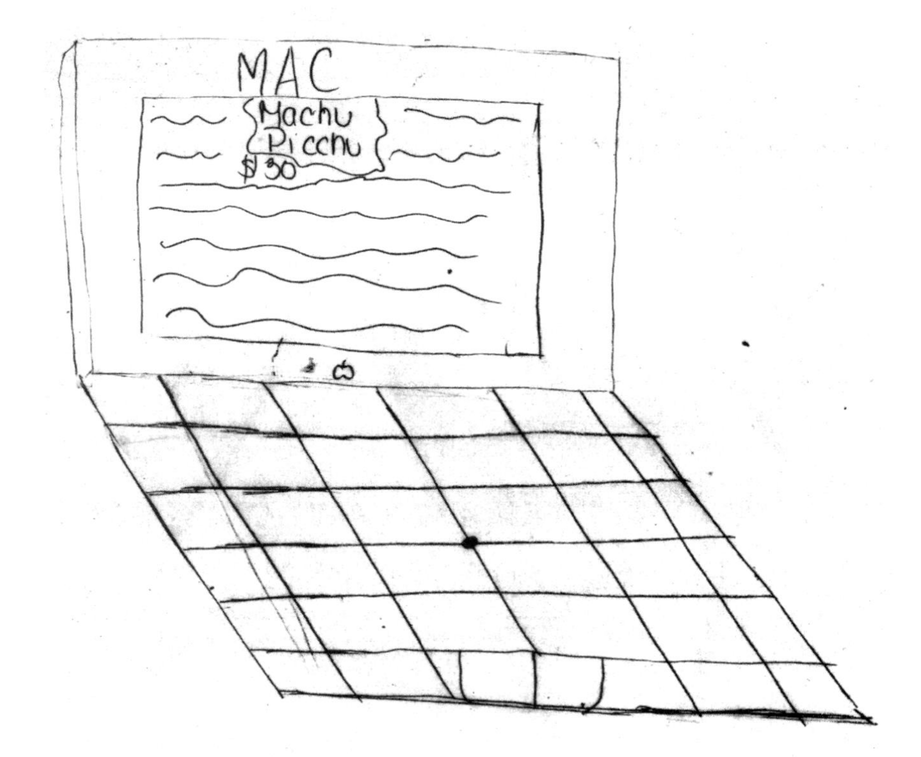

Illustration Credit: Courtney Siegel and Brittany Neely

A Message from the Teacher, Mrs. Ellen Schwartz

The making of *Matthew's Tangled Trails* can be compared to gardening. Planting the seeds, cultivating the young minds of my students, and watching them grow tall with blossoms facing the sun, can only bring a teacher the greatest of pleasures.

The process of writing, like gardening, is never an easy task. Working on *Matthew's Tangled Trails* and seeing my student's growth while learning so much more than what is on the written page, empowered all of us. The process of sharing ideas, thoughts, and criticisms is invaluable. The lessons learned as well as discussions and debates dealing with everyday teenage problems was infinitely worthwhile. The forum afforded the students the opportunity to delve into their own feelings and arrive at viable solutions.

Writing, re-writing, and editing, and the entire creative process was a course of its own. Can a teacher ask for more when all aspects of learning are going on and the end product is not only *Matthew's Tangled Trails*, but the smiles of accomplishment on the faces of such wonderful students?

I was thankful for the opportunity to help prepare these young people for the arena of "life" with this small step, hopeful they will take many giant ones in the future.

Illustration Credit: Ian Li

What did you like best about writing *Matthew's Tangled Trails?*

I enjoyed experiencing what a real author does when writing a novel.
Andrew Bank

The best part was the satisfaction of having my name in a quality piece of writing.
Flynn Hill

Knowing that a book I was part of is going to be published.
Zach Coppola

Creating our own nightmares and endings.
Ian Li

The best thing I liked about *Matthew's Tangled Trails* was the freedom to change it.
Douglas Gibbons

We were writing our own book, using our ideas, and having a say and an opinion.
Courtney Siegel

What I liked best about writing *Matthew's Tangled Trails* was how one way led to another, and how we got to write the ending just the way we wanted.
Hailey Simon

I liked the idea of being able to have a once-in-a-lifetime chance to write a book.
Jason Shilling

I was able to control how the story ended, and knew the ending of the book before anyone else!
Laura Lupo

It was a good book and good mystery, but it also taught you something - how scamming is wrong and to be very careful on the internet.
Sofia-Marie Guttilla

We got to decide what gets put into the book and if we didn't like something it could be changed.
Dalia Gaon

Maybe kids can learn about bullying from the people in the book.
Lindsay Melworm

Seeing the story of a Hispanic boy trying to fit in.
Cesar Gonzalez

It was very interesting to see how hard it is to write a book, and how authors go through a lot.
Amanda Burnett

I felt like I was in charge. I actually had a say in how the book was written. I really feel like an author.
Shaun Werbelow

I liked that all of our ideas contributed to the book, and we got a lot of say in all the parts.
Brittany Neely

I enjoyed creating a solution to the mystery, meeting with my group, and discussing the characters and plot.
Caitlin Isham

Our ideas were transformed into a 150-page book. In addition, I had the power to change anything in the book that I wanted.
Landon Marder

I liked editing all of the grammar and punctuation like a real editor.
Allison Saltzman

I liked the feeling that I was in control of the book, and that people will actually read my work.
Nicole Taykhman

I liked writing the nightmare best. I thought it was fun because we could make Matthew dream whatever we wanted.
Kimberly Gurock

The thing I liked best was the feeling that you know a published book has your contributions.
Arielle Richheimer

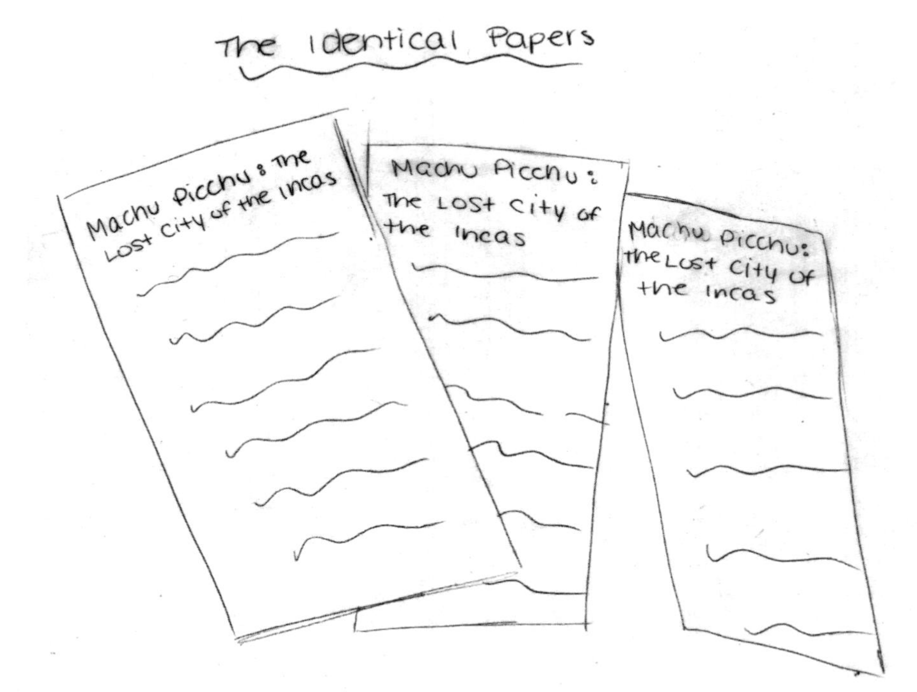

Illustration Credit: Brittany Neely

Illustration Credit: Nicole Taykhman

Matthew's "Other" Nightmares

Matthew is walking down a long hallway. There are many doors, all different shapes, sizes and colors. He keeps walking and decides to open a door. It is a swirling door, colored all in red. He walks in and there is "Eddie's Scam" written in big letters on a table. He slams the door and tries another . . . going to many more horrific doors until there is only one left. He opens it and then . . . wakes up.
Danielle Schwarz

Run, run, run, have to escape! This was going through Matthew's mind as he ran down a tunnel. He was running from all his problems - the invisible cybercrook laughing at him, Mike's words . . . just running from the worst of his problems.
Rebecca Vedrin

Matthew was walking and he saw a glob of ketchup on the floor. He grabbed a damp towel and wiped it off the floor. The floor was nice and clean. He went to put the towel back where he got it when he noticed the ketchup had returned to the floor. It seemed to spell something out, "Eddies' Scam." Matthew started running in the opposite direction of the ketchup.
Jordon Wolfson

Matthew is running down a never-ending street. Everyone is chasing him, led by Mike. They are all in a big mob with pitchfork, torches, and knives. As Matthew is running he passes the Blitz. It is all trashed. In big blood letters on the window a note says "Matthew's Scam."
Mike Karp

I go to the school. Suddenly I see Mr. Richie being beaten up by Mike and his bystanders. There's something from Mr. Richie's desk. It looks like a piece of paper - *Eddie's paper!* I run over to try to stop Mike but he sees me and starts talking trash. Mike takes out a gun and holds it to my head, laughing out loud.
Zack Ehrlich

Matthew falls asleep and pictures of Eddie being bullied, Mike bullying him, and Matthew becoming the next victim, flash through his mind. The words run through his head, "I don't believe this is happening, how did he get my paper?" Blank disks are flying through his dreams and Matthew is finally hit with one, waking up in a cold sweat.
Bennett Siegel

Matthew walks into Mr. Richie's class just as the bell rings.
"Good news, class," Mr. Richie begins, we've discovered who the cybercrook is."
Whispers spread throughout the classroom and eyes dart to Eddie, who just smiles.
"Matthew," Mr. Richie continues, "please return the money now."
Mr. Richie and the rest of the class chant Matthew's name as they close in on him.
Julie Mintz

The crowd of bystanders took action. They were all on top of Matthew. Unfortunately, Mike was right near him and he was throwing punches at Matthew. The next thing he knew, Eddie, Nicole, and Gizmo were all included in the massacre of Matthew. "Help, help," Matthew screamed. There was nothing he could do. It was the worse moment of his life. Everybody turned on him. Luckily, a miracle happened. The alarm rang: 6:45. Matthew woke up from a horrible nightmare.
Jordan Schneider

Matthew fell into a deep sleep. He had the worst nightmare ever. He was running away down a never-ending hall as Eddie, Mike, Kyle, JC, and Dan chased him. Then Jenna popped up and Matthew saw a blank face sending a paper on the computer. He was terrified. He fell into a big hole where Mr. Richie was screaming at him. Matthew's hair was sticking straight up. Matthew woke up, shaking and taking deep breaths.
Arielle Richheimer

Matthew was walking through school when he saw Eddie, white as a ghost, with Mike standing in front of him, fists clenched tight. Eddie's head fell to the side and was looking at Matthew. Mike quickly spun around - Mike had red eyes and horns!! Mike smiled, showed razor-sharp teeth, pounced at Matthew, and then ran off on all fours.
Matt Cohen

I'm a spider, crawling up my web. I am searching for a way out, crawling quickly but carefully so I do not fall. I look down stupidly, only to see my good friend Eddie staring up at me. "Help," Eddie's eyes say. I do not go down because I must reach the top of my web. I look up only to see another person staring down at me. Mike, the bully, intimidator, and leader, has an angry look in his eyes. I get scared; I fear the top of the web. What should I do? Before I can decide, I see bright light. Suddenly I wake up, sweating.
Andrew Bank

Illustration Credit: Chelsea Fitzgerald and Kimberly Gurock

Illustration Credit: Sofia-Marie Guttila

Bully Stories from the Student Authors

There was a bully who always had two followers behind him. Everyday, the kids played in the park. The bully went around pushing people. My friends and I hated this. Whenever we went to the park, we got pushed into the fences. Finally, one parent had enough. She went up to the father of the bully and yelled at him. Surprisingly, the father didn't know about what was happening. We didn't see the bully at the park for a while. When he finally came back, he didn't have any followers. He never pushed anyone against the fences again.

A girl who used to be my friend started spreading rumors about all my friends and me. She is insecure and doesn't have many friends. She thinks I steal her friends from her. She is teased, so I think that she has low self-esteem and just wants attention. The rumors might be her way to deal with her insecurity.

During elementary school I was the shortest kid in my grade. Eventually, I got used to getting teased about being short. They called me short, tiny, midget, shrimp, etc. When I came to Middle School there was a whole new crowd of people to deal with. My solution was to classify myself as "vertically challenged." If I'm still short when I finish growing up, I'll classify myself as "vertically impaired."

There was a girl who was short, fat, and all she wanted was to fit in with a certain group of kids. She tried to dress like them, wearing the same clothes, shoes, and jewelry that everyone wore! She tried to talk with them, but they just ignored her. She became depressed, but would not give up. The harder she tried, the more the other girls disliked her. She spent all her parent's money on trends. No matter what she did, she always felt different. The girls all whispered and laughed at her! So she just gave up, became herself, and before she knew it, made different friends that she liked even better.

A boy was made fun of all the time. Once, another boy put peanut butter (which he is allergic to) on his nose! The boy would always play with his imaginary friends. He complained that all the other boys always teased him. Then he met a friend. His friend came over to his house a lot. Soon, he met two new friends. Even though he only has three school friends, that's enough for the other kids to lay off him. They see he's more confident. So the kids that picked on him found a new target.

Illustration Credit: Doug Witzenbocker

Group Solutions

The student-authors were put into groups to "pool" their ideas. The hardest part of their work was finding a group name! Group members collaborated on a solution to the mystery. The following are their results:

Dylan did it because of revenge. He was mad at Eddie because he got more hours than him at the Blitz.
Slackmills

Matthew headed for the Blitz. Matthew noticed that Mike was paying with one-dollar bills marked in red, in his handwriting. Matthew realized he had just found the cybercrook.
Fantastic 4+1

Nicole and Matthew noticed a tall stack of papers on Mr. Richie's desk. It was Eddie's paper. Matthew lifted up each piece of paper, expecting to find his own paper in the stack, but he only found more copies. Mr. Richie walked into the classroom. "I am the culprit," Mr. Richie said, revealing the truth.
The No Names

"Dylan did it," Matthew said to Mr. Richie. "He sold everyone the research papers online. I marked my money on wheresgeorge.com and at the Burger Blitz, Dylan was paying with one of my bills."
The Spirit Fairies

Sara confessed everything - wanting to give better presents to Mike than the other girls, (specifically Breanna), and stealing Eddie's disk. She also confessed that Dylan was promised a part of the proceeds for finding things out about each house for the customized e-mail (yes, it was Dylan who sneaked around in the bushes).
Scuba Squad

Nicole went to the library and saw a kid with a dollar bill on the

computer website, wheresgeorge.com. She recognized him as Dylan and spotted Matthew's handwriting on the bill.
2 Guys, 2 Girls, and A Manuscript

Mr. Richie announced to the class that he was the scammer. He did it to show them how wrong bullying is, and about how groups are not ways of protection and taking charge.
HKKIMD

"It's Dylan," Matthew screamed. "The disk was stolen at the library." Dylan registered the wheresgeorge.com dollar from a person named Nalyd (Dylan spelled backwards).
B.R.A.D.

Jenna wedged herself between Mike and Eddie. It was too late. Mike had already thrown a punch with great force into Jenna. She fell backwards and went crashing into the concrete. A floppy disk and one of Matthew's marked dollars flew out of her pocket.
D.A.L.J.S.

Dylan put his hand in the mailbox, took an envelope and ran. "Caught!!" Matthew said to himself.
The Fruit Cakes

Kyle wrote an "I'm sorry" e-mail:
"I want to apologize for the scam I used on you. My mother is single and can't afford the treatment that my 2-year-old brother needs for his Leukemia. I just wanted my brother to live. I'll think of a better way to help. I'm soooo sorry!
By Myself

They heard a boy's voice muttering, and an occasional strong punch on a pillow. Then Dylan sat down and told his story.
The Dodo Birds + A Girl

Different Consequences

Choosing the punishment is a difficult decision. The severity of the crime must be weighed against the damage it created. Here are some sentences imposed by the student-authors.

The cybercrook was forced to take the final and no one else had to. She got a 75 and had to go to summer school. She lost her friends because she did something so stupid.
Abby Cohen

The cybercrook was expelled from school so she couldn't do it ever again.
Evan Massa

She was suspended, fined, and got a criminal record.
John O'Sullivan

The cybercrook was punished by having to give the money back. She was suspended for two weeks, had to do community service, and help out after school.
Chelsea Fitzgerald

He was suspended from school, kicked off the paper, and forced to clean the crazy bus driver's bus.
Shaun Werbelow

The cybercrook was sent to Juvenile Hall.
Matt Cohen

The cybercrook was sentenced to a year's worth of community service, and jail.
Mike Karp

The cybercrook begged everyone not to get into trouble. She gave back the money then fessed up. Mr. Richie gave her a small

suspension.
Landon Marder

She had to give back all the money, and then went around the school giving lectures on how bad internet scams are.
Laura Lupo

The cybercrook got 52.5 hours of community service and was suspended from school.
Flynn Hill

She had to write her own report without using a computer, and automatically start with 15 points off.
Katherine DiMaggio

She had to give back the money, apologize to everyone she affected, get points taken off her social studies paper, and clean the crazy bus driver's bus.
Lisa Gurock

The cybercrook was punished by having to hand wash the crazy bus driver's clothes (including socks).
Zach Coppola

The cybercrook was suspended, failed social studies, kicked off the newspaper, and had to give all the money back plus 25%.
Max Levy

He was suspended from school, forced to make up the time missed during his suspension at summer school, kicked off the newspaper, and had to re-do his paper.
Allison Saltzman

She was suspended, fined, and got a criminal record.
John O'Sullivan

Quick Guide to Important Websites

School Website
www.bellmore-merrick.k12.ny.us/merrickave/index.html

Anti-bullying Websites
www.antibullying.net
www.bullybeware.com
www.nea.org/issues/safescho/bullying/
www.stopbullyingnow.com

Books by Teens
www.booksbyteens.com

Internet Safety Websites
www.safekids.com
www.safeteens.com
www.yahooligans.com/docs/safety
www.GetNetwise.org
www.isafe.org

Plagiarism
www.ehhs.cmich.edu/~mspears/plagiarism.html
www.2learn.ca/mapset/SafetyNet/plagiarism/Plagiarismresources.html

Illustration Credit: Jordan Wolfson

Meet the Student Authors

Who are the student authors of *Matthew's Tangled Trails?* The fifty-five seventh graders who participated are all students in Mrs. Schwartz's honors classes at Merrick Avenue Middle School (MAMS). There are almost 1000 students in the two grades, 7th and 8th, at MAMS. They live in Merrick, a suburb that lies about thirty miles east of New York City. Merrick is located on the south shore of Long Island, a short ride away from the famous Jones Beach. The name of the town means "peaceful", derived from a local Indian tribe, the *Meroke*.

To learn more about these talented young people, *Books by Teens* conducted before-and-after surveys. Here are the results.

Bullying in MAMS is a problem, similar to other schools around the *world*. More than one out of every two students report being bullied. Merrick teens usually handle a bully by ignoring him or her, telling a teacher or staff person, or fighting back. Amanda Pechman says that she would first ignore the bully and then, if it didn't work, fight back verbally. Her classmate, Brittany Clahane notes that she would "try to stick up for people who are bullied."

Nearly all the student authors wish they could stop kids from picking on one another. However, 44% are not sure it's really possible. 8 out of 10 kids believe that schools should teach students how to control bullies. E-bullying is a different matter. "I know of people who have been mistreated online," a student wrote, "and they don't even know who they're talking to." Less than 60% of the kids were not exactly sure what an e-bully was before they worked on *Matthew's Tangled Trails*. By the time they were finished, 100% could recognize an e-bully and the potential danger of meeting one online.

Similarly, working on the book dramatically changed teen's attitudes toward buying papers on the internet. 25% of the students felt it was okay before writing *Matthew's Tangled Trails*; after the project was completed a resounding 94% said it was wrong. Bryan Brown described the experience of collaborating on a published book very simply. "What I liked best about the book," he wrote, "was that we had the power to change things."

Meet Jeri Fink and Donna Paltrowitz

Jeri Fink and Donna Paltrowitz are long-time friends and neighbors who have worked together on many projects. They developed the *Books By Teens* series because they believe that teenagers should be active participants in the choices they make.

Jeri Fink: Dr. Jeri Fink is a practicing family therapist, journalist, and author of fiction and nonfiction books. Her work explores, among other subjects, how technology affects our behavior and our relationships to one another. Dr. Fink lives in New York with her husband, dog, cat, and near her two grown sons and seven very special nieces and nephews. Dr. Fink also lives with, and trains her labradoodle, Gizmo.

Donna Paltrowitz: Donna Paltrowitz is an educator who, along with her husband, Stuart Paltrowitz, has co-authored over sixty children's books and software programs. Their work explores the many social, emotional, and educational issues faced by kids today. Mrs. Paltrowitz lives in New York with her husband and three children.